REUNITED
BY THE
GREEK'S VOWS

ANDIE BROCK

MILLS & BOON

First published in Great Britain 2019
by Mills & Boon, an imprint of HarperCollins*Publishers*
1 London Bridge Street, London, SE1 9GF

Large Print edition 2019

© 2019 Andrea Brock

ISBN: 978-0-263-08287-6

MIX
Paper from
responsible sources
FSC™ C007454

This book is produced from independently certified FSC™ paper to ensure responsible forest management. For more information visit www.harpercollins.co.uk/green.

Printed and bound in Great Britain
by CPI Group (UK) Ltd, Croydon, CR0 4YY

For Hil. With much love.

CHAPTER ONE

KATE FROZE, THE bottle of champagne foaming in her hand. *Oh, please no! Not him—not here!* She screwed up her eyes, praying that when she opened them again he would have miraculously vanished. But, no. He was still there, and the shock of his presence was ringing in her ears, blotting out everyone else in the room.

Watching as if in slow motion horror, Kate saw him lean back to address the overly attentive waitress. Broodingly handsome, all sculpted features and olive skin, his broad shoulders and towering height were carried with that familiar, athletic grace. Nikos Nikoladis. Her first love. Her ex-fiancé. The man who had broken her heart.

'Hey, honey, careful with that champagne.' A diner at Kate's table reached out to steady her hand. 'If you knew what it cost you might treat it with a bit more respect.'

As the other men snickered in agreement

Kate forced herself to apologise, holding a rictus grin that threatened to break her jaw as she refilled their glasses. She didn't know exactly what it cost, but she did know it was a vastly over-inflated price, designed to feed their self-importance rather than please their palates. The enormous egos and choking testosterone of the herd of fat-cat businessmen here tonight made it hard to breathe.

But that was why she was here. Why she had signed up to this agency specialising in corporate hospitality. Why she had wriggled into a short black skirt that barely covered her butt and the horrible faux leather waistcoat now pulling tight across her bust. Because if there was the slightest chance that she might be able to persuade one of these arrogant jerks to invest in her ailing family business then she was going to take it. And if that meant she had to play waitress at this godawful event, flirt a little with these people, massage their massive egos, then so be it. As long as they knew that was the only thing she'd be massaging.

Because desperate times called for desperate measures. And, boy, was Kate desperate. And that had been even before the mortifying reappearance of her ex-fiancé.

Lowering her head, she let a curtain of blonde hair fall across her face, then took another peek in his direction, refusing to acknowledge the quickening of her heart. Engrossed in conversation with the CEO of a major corporation on his left, Nikos didn't appear to have spotted her. That, at least, was some consolation. And he wasn't seated at one of her designated tables in this vast hotel dining room, for which she was supremely grateful.

With a bit of luck she might be able keep her back to him and avoid being seen. Her new hairstyle would help her—the tumbling blonde curls were very different from the sleek mane of chestnut hair belonging to the Kate he had once known.

Refusing to panic, Kate squashed down her instinct to turn tail and run. Much as she wanted to tell the agency what they could do with their sleazy job, its degrading outfit and its horrible, predatory guests, the fact was that even if trying to persuade one of them to invest in Kandy Kate *was* a ludicrously naïve idea, this was still

well-paid work with the potential for healthy tips
and she needed the money.

There were over three hundred diners here tonight, and at least thirty waitresses. As long as
she kept her wits about her she should be able to
avoid Nikos. She *would* avoid him. Because coming face to face with him when she was dressed
like a backstreet hooker was one humiliation she
could firmly do without.

What was he even *doing* here? She shot him
another surreptitious glance from beneath heavy
lashes. She would never have put Nikos down
as the sort of man who would attend this type
of do—even if it *was* a charity event. But then
she would never have thought he was the kind
of guy to rip her life apart the way he had. To be
capable of such abject cruelty. She had no idea
who Nikos really was at all.

What she *did* know was that she had totally
lost her heart to this man. To the gorgeous Greek
Adonis who had waited on her table that warm
summer's evening in Crete three long years ago.
The handsome, charming, captivating stranger
who had walked along the beach with her, taking her hand, kissing her under the stars, turning
her upside down and inside out there and then

with a crazy sort of love that she'd thought only existed in stories.

That summer had been the most wonderful time of her life. And the hurt that had followed more excruciating than she would ever have imagined possible.

So why was she surprised that he would frequent this sort of event? He was certainly wealthy enough. In fact, he could probably buy out most of these guys and scarcely make a dent in his multi-billion-dollar fortune.

Kate had watched his meteoric rise to enormous wealth from afar. The carefree, laid-back guy she'd fallen in love with, who hadn't had two cents to rub together when she'd met him, had become a billionaire businessman almost overnight. In the blink of a red-rimmed eye.

Whereas, of course, *her* fortunes had done the reverse. Her family's well-established confectionery business, Kandy Kate, had been crippled by a series of bad decisions since her father had died. But Kate was absolutely determined that was going to change. She was going to save Kandy Kate if it was the last thing she did. Because it was her father's legacy, named in her honour. It had meant everything to him. And for that reason it meant everything to her.

'Hey, baby, I'm dying of thirst over here!'

More raucous laughter around the table snapped Kate back to the job she was supposed to be doing.

'Get that pretty little ass of yours around here and refill my glass.'

'Yes, sir, of course.' Silently seething, Kate cautiously sidled around the table, keeping her back to Nikos as best she could.

'Whassup, honey? You scared of me?' The man stretched out his arm, snaking it around Kate's waist to pull her closer. ''Cos you know, there ain't no need for that. I'm nice as pie. You ask anyone.' More drunken hee-hawing. 'Why don't you come sit on my lap and I'll show you just how *nice* I can be?'

Taking a step back, Kate gripped the neck of the champagne bottle tightly enough to throttle it. It was a poor substitute for what she would have *liked* to throttle, but it would have to do.

'I'm not paid to sit down.' She feigned a light-hearted remark through gritted teeth.

'No? Well, I'm sure we could make it worth your while. Whaddya you say, guys?'

The man lurched forward, knocking Kate off balance so that she stumbled, falling towards him. She tried to right herself, to pull away, but he was too strong for her and before she knew it he had tugged her firmly down onto his lap, spreading his legs to accommodate her, his alcohol-soaked breath belching into her face. And when he adjusted his position, pressing her down onto his crotch, she genuinely thought she was going to be sick.

No job was worth this. No amount of money would compensate for being treated like a piece of meat.

For God's sake Kate, she told herself, dragging in a breath, *have a bit of self-respect.*

But she mustn't make a scene. The last thing she wanted to do was draw attention to herself— not with Nikos across the other side of the room. Extricating herself as carefully as possible, her stomach roiling as her movement only served to arouse her captor more, she put the champagne bottle down on the table and started to lever herself away from him.

'Oh, no, you don't.' He pulled her back down, his foul breath in her ear. 'I'm just startin' to enjoy myself. You can probably tell…'

* * *

From the other side of the glittering dining room, Nikos narrowed his eyes, turning in his chair to get a better look. Something about that young woman was very familiar, making him stare long and hard. Making his pulse beat faster too, if he would but admit it. It couldn't be...could it?

He'd watched as she moved around her table, filling the glasses of rowdy guests who had already had way too much. With her back to him, and quite some distance away, he didn't have much to go on—and the mane of blonde curls was telling him he must be mistaken. But as he'd watched she had raised a hand to touch her earlobe, tugging on it gently in an unconscious display of vulnerability the way he had seen her do a hundred times before.

And then Nikos had known without a shadow of doubt.

It was her.

Kate O'Connor.

He'd sat back in his chair, waiting for his heart-rate to steady. *Of all the gin joints...* It almost felt as if he'd conjured her up from his mind. Because Kate O'Connor had been very much on his mind lately. Hadn't he had just flown five thousand miles to see her? The prospect of ambushing her in her office the following morning had brought him a twisted sort of pleasure that had made the journey almost enjoyable.

And now here she was, right in front of him, a vision in tart's clothing. Never would he have expected to find Kate in a place like this, looking like that. He wouldn't be here himself if he hadn't been talked into it by a business associate who had insisted they would talk shop over dinner. One look at the place and he'd almost turned around there and then. But something had made him stay. It must have been a sixth sense.

Unable to tear his gaze way, Nikos had watched on as one guy had slid an arm around Kate's waist, pulling her closer. He'd felt his hands ball into fists. *Steady, now.* This was none of his business. Maybe it was all part of the service.

He had waited for some sense of satisfaction to kick in, for a feeling of gratification at seeing what Kate had been reduced to to warm his dry bones. But, strangely, there was none to be had. Nikos could find no consolation in her downfall.

He wanted to. Badly. He wanted to enjoy every minute of this degrading spectacle—to revel in it and to feel it thawing the very core of him. A core that had hardened like stone in the years since their bitter break-up.

But now, as he watched her sliding onto some creep's lap, the emotion rising in his gullet had nothing to do with comfort or consolation. It was pure rage—so bitter and acrid that it burnt his throat with its vicious bile.

Because Kate O'Connor was his. Or at least she soon would be.

Downing the last of his whisky in one burning gulp, Nikos forced himself to calm down. His every instinct was screaming at him to cross the room, haul Kate off the lap of that revolting sleazeball, fling her over his shoulder and carry her out of this place.

His body positively twitched with the effort of stopping himself. But stop himself he would. Because Nikos was cleverer than that. He was here to claim his ex-fiancée and finally she would do his bidding. She just didn't know it yet. But right now, it was time to leave.

Back in her tiny apartment, Kate sprawled down on the bed, burying her face in the covers. That had been one of the most humiliating nights of her life—and lately she'd had a few.

Pulling herself upright, she shifted along the bed and swung her legs over the end, leaning forward to prop her elbows on the top of the dresser. This place was so small that during her first week there she'd had to battle against claustrophobic panic attacks in the middle of the night.

But that had long since passed and she had become used to it. Her spacious penthouse condominium at the top of KK Towers—her family home before it had all gone so badly wrong—was now not much more than a distant memory.

She peered at herself in the mirror, wincing at the sight that met her eyes. She hardly recognised the heavily made-up blonde who stared back at her—which was all to the good. Because that person wasn't her. She was just a means to an end. An end that couldn't come fast enough for Kate.

Raising her hand, she grasped a fistful of hair and lifted up the blonde wig, tossing it to one side. She shook her head, running her fingers through her short dark hair before regarding herself again. Better. She had worn this style for over a year now, her decision to crop her long chestnut hair having been an attempt to present a more businesslike, serious persona.

The business might still bear her name, but Kate was no longer the happy, rosy-cheeked kid who had promoted the brand throughout her childhood—whose chestnut plaits and gap-toothed smile had helped to sell several million candy bars and made Kate instantly recognisable.

Now Kate was all grown up. And as head of the Kandy Kate empire it fell to her to stop the rot and save the company. To keep production running. Which meant generating the cash flow needed to pay their suppliers. And looking after the staff—some of whom had been with the company right from the start, who were more like family.

They were loyal employees, who had stood by Kandy Kate through bad times and even worse times, taking a salary cut, sometimes no salary at all, because they had loved her dad. Because they had faith that Kate would get the company back on track…see them right.

And Kate was absolutely determined she wasn't going to let them down. Somehow she was going to save Kandy Kate—even if she didn't have a clue how she was going to do it.

Peeling off the hateful false eyelashes, she

blinked with relief, then set about scrubbing away her heavy make-up before heading for the shower. She felt soiled, unclean, and the pummelling hot water was doing nothing to remove the scent of the evening that seemed to have crept under her skin, into her pores. But at least she had managed to stick it out until the end, so that would mean she'd get paid.

And, more importantly, she had avoided being recognised by Nikos. That alone made her awful disguise worthwhile.

After finally managing to extricate herself from that creep's lap, she had shot a panicked glance in Nikos's direction, sick with dread that he might have witnessed the humiliating scene. But to her immense relief he had gone—vanished. A quick, hopeful glance around her revealed no sign of him, and when his seat had still been empty twenty minutes later Kate had finally let herself breathe.

She had got away with it. Because if Nikos had recognised her he wouldn't have been able to resist storming over, nailing her with those piercing ebony eyes and watching her squirm with embarrassment. Gloating over how the mighty had fallen.

Because fall she had—from a great height. After Kate's father had died she and her mother had been left in joint control of Kandy Kate, and between them they had brought the business to its knees. The combination of Fiona O'Connor's erratic decisions and Kate's naivety had rapidly turned the thriving, much-loved brand—a household name—into a company on the brink of bankruptcy.

Too late Kate had realised that her mother wasn't mentally strong enough to have taken on such a weighty responsibility. But by then the Kandy Kate name had already been dragged through the mud—no longer associated with traditional values and a wholesome image but rocked by indiscreet comments from the new boss.

Convinced she knew best, Fiona had waltzed into the office on her first day like an impending storm, immediately making ridiculous demands and crazy decisions. The board had tried to overrule her, but Fiona would have none of it, convinced that they were just being obstructive because they didn't like her. It had got so bad that anyone who'd tried to stand up to her had been fired on the spot, with senior executives told to clear their desks there and then.

As the carnage had continued Kate had begged her mother to step down, to leave the running of the company to *her*—for the sake of Fiona's mental health as well as for the business. But as it had turned out leaving Kandy Kate in her hands had been even worse. Failing to keep a check on the new finance director—appointed by Fiona after the previous one had walked out in protest—Kate had signed papers without looking at them properly and delegated power to him, completely unaware of his fraudulent intentions.

Gullibility, lack of experience, and the fact that Kate had been way out of her depth had cost the company dear. Within months the con man had syphoned off vast quantities of money, leaving Kandy Kate in a more desperate state than ever.

Nearly three years had passed since then, and Kate had wised up considerably. But despite her best efforts—despite selling off just about every asset that Kandy Kate had had left, working all the hours that God sent, begging, borrowing and pleading with banks, investors, and anyone else who might be prepared to pour some serious capital into the business—Kate had got nowhere.

The sad fact was that Kate's eponymous business was still in a dire state. And, short of a miracle, there was nothing she could do to repair it.

The press, of course, were lapping it up. Fiona O'Connor had always been good tabloid fodder, with her expensive tastes and her erratic outbursts. But, as the face of Kandy Kate, Kate herself was the real prize. Hounded by the press all her life, she never knew when she was going to be snapped by a lone pap, hoping to make a few dollars out of her—though why anyone should be remotely interested in seeing her buying a few groceries in the local deli or snatching a coffee on her way to work she had no idea.

Events like the Executives' Club, however, were a different matter. Which was why Kate made sure she concealed her identity with a false name, a blonde wig and more make-up than a three-year-old at a clown convention.

Getting into bed, she pulled the covers under her chin.

Maybe it was time to give up. This morning she'd discovered there had been a surge in the price of Kandy Kate's shares, and that meant only one thing. Someone was planning a hostile takeover. Which was all she needed.

Kate had hoped she might be able to glean some information as to who might be behind the takeover from some of guests at the Executives' Club. Obviously she'd had to make sure she didn't reveal who she was, but successful businessmen loved to brag and champagne loosened their tongues. Unfortunately it also loosened their hands, and Kate had found them far more interested in stroking her butt or staring down her cleavage than giving her the lowdown on the latest gossip from the trading floor.

Closing her eyes, Kate willed herself to go to sleep. She was dog-tired...physically and emotionally drained. But sleep refused to come. Instead, Nikos's powerful image filled her vision, crowding her mind, snapping her eyes open again.

The acute shock of seeing him tonight still held her body in a rigid grip. The three years since she had last seen him had vanished like vapour the second she had set eyes on him again. One glance at that handsome face and the memories of their break-up had come flooding back: the fight, the things they had said...horrible, hateful, brutal words...all recalled with vivid clarity. She felt as if time had simply distilled the pain, making it even more potent as it sank its vicious claws into her once again.

When Nikos had left her, Kate's whole world had collapsed. Her hopes and dreams had crumbled before her eyes—built, as it turned out, on nothing more substantial than the shifting sands of blind optimism and unguarded love. She had fallen into a place so deep, so dark, that she had feared she would never see the light again.

But somehow she had clawed her way back up. Somehow she had survived.

As she stared up at the peeling paintwork of the ceiling Kate conceded that their relationship had been doomed from the start. The cracks had always been there—just ignored in the first wild rush of all-consuming passion. A time when anything had seemed possible.

She hadn't been totally blameless. By choosing to play down her family's wealth and lavish lifestyle she had been guilty of deceiving Nikos. It had been a selfish act, but the relief of being free from the shackles of Kandy Kate that had dominated her whole life had been so wonderful, so liberating, she had lied by omission just to try and keep it that way for as long as possible.

Just for a while she had wanted to be Kate

O'Connor—a regular kind of girl from an ordinary background, who happened to have been fortunate enough to fall in love with the most wonderful guy in the world.

But the flipside had meant she'd failed to mention Nikos to her parents. Far less the fact that she had rushed headlong into an engagement with him. That she intended to marry the remarkable Greek man as soon as possible.

Because Kate had known full well the ruckus it would cause. She knew her mother would hit the roof and insist that the engagement was broken off immediately—that there was no way she was going to allow her daughter to marry some penniless Greek bum. And then her poor father would be dragged into it, torn between the two women in his life the way he always was, doing his best to keep the peace.

Kate had decided that she was going to keep the engagement a secret for as long as she could. But when news had arrived that her father had been taken seriously ill her little secret had suddenly begun to grow, to take on a life of its own.

As she'd rushed to make plans to return to New York Nikos had assumed he would be going with her. But Kate hadn't been able to let that happen. Her parents hadn't even known of his existence—she couldn't arrive back home with him by her side, knowing the way her mother would react and risking damaging her father's fragile health still further.

So she had insisted Nikos stayed behind in Crete. She could still remember the look of hurt on his face when she'd told him. Standing there in the Greek sunshine, so tall and proud, his dark brows pulling together in surprise, his features had set like stone.

It had all but broken her heart, but Kate had stood firm, slinging her rucksack over her shoulder and turning away when all she'd wanted to do was to fall into his arms and stay there for ever.

If she had come clean there and then, confessed everything, would things have turned out differently?

Kate had gone over that moment in her head a thousand times. But the fact was she hadn't. And as Nikos's hurt had quickly turned to a carefully controlled anger, a cold cloud of animosity had descended over them as they'd said their goodbyes.

Nikos's dry peck on her cheek had only accentuated the widening rift between them.

Her father had died two weeks later. And in the melee of trying to organise everything—taking care of her mother, who had always suffered from fragile mental health, as well as coping with her own crippling grief—suddenly Nikos had arrived. Unannounced. Uninvited. And even though her heart had leapt at the sight of him—even though he had been the person Kate had wanted to see more than anyone else in the world, *needed* more than anyone else in the world—she had panicked.

Hadn't she expressly told him not to come? His arrival was going to cause nothing but trouble. And that trouble had started almost immediately.

Within minutes her guilty secret had been exposed. Dropping his bag, Nikos had looked around the luxurious apartment with a puzzled expression on his face before pulling her into a stiff hug.

With immaculate timing Fiona O'Connor had walked in at that precise moment, demanding to know who this *person* was. And as Nikos had stepped forward to offer his condolences, and to introduce himself as Kate's fiancé, she had let out a little scream, her hand fluttering to her throat.

Kate had had no choice but to try and do whatever she could to mitigate the damage, to calm Fiona down. Even though that had meant pushing Nikos away.

And then, on that last evening—the evening of her father's funeral—her whole shaky world had finally collapsed.

When she'd been at her lowest ebb Nikos had turned on her, slashing through her battered defences, inflicting the sort of crippling pain from which there was no recovery…

Turning on her side, Kate curled herself into a ball as the memory of how Nikos had looked tonight imprinted itself on her brain. Gone had been the laid-back guy she had once known, casually dressed in faded jeans slung low on his hips or board shorts frayed at the hems by the sun and the sea. Gone the mass of wind-blown dark curls. Now his hair was tamed, styled, carefully groomed like the rest of him. Now he wore a dinner suit with the easy confidence of a wealthy man, giving off an air of urbane arrogance that told the world he had made it, that life was his for the taking.

Feeling a stab of pain, she buried her head in her pillow. Not for the first time she conceded that Nikos was the one man who had the wealth and the contacts to save her precious business. But there was no way she would ask him. She might only have a shred of pride left, but she was damned if she was going to give that shred to him. No, hell would freeze over before she *ever* went crawling to him.

CHAPTER TWO

NIKOS GAZED UP at KK Towers, an imposing glass-fronted building in Midtown Manhattan. He had been surprised to discover that the Kandy Kate headquarters were still located here. From what he'd heard, all the offices and apartments had been leased off, even if the premises still retained the KK name.

Christened by Bernie O'Connor, it had been a glittering symbol of the power and success of the Kandy Kate empire, with its offices sprawling over several floors and the stunning penthouse apartment home to his adored family.

He had never met Bernie, but he had obviously been an astute businessman—something that Nikos respected highly. To have made such a success of the Kandy Kate business in what had to be a very competitive market took intelligence and guts.

It was a shame he hadn't applied those same principles to his private life. From what Nikos could see, Bernie had made completely the wrong choice of wife.

Fiona O'Connor was an arrogant snob—that much had been obvious from the start. Her rudeness Nikos might have accepted. After all, when they had met Fiona had been recently bereaved…he would have made allowances. He could even have excused her blatant hostility, given the circumstances. Particularly in light of the fact that Kate had conveniently forgotten to tell her mother of his existence. But the way she had looked at him with such abject horror—as if he was worse than nothing—*that* had got under his skin.

And then there was Kate…

Nikos held his jaw firm as he marched through the revolving doors into a light-filled vestibule. What right did he have to criticise Bernie O'Connor about his choice of partner when he had made the same mistake—with bells on? He too had fallen for totally the wrong woman.

The 'Kate effect' had hit Nikos like a tornado. His golden rule of never getting emotionally involved with any woman had been smashed just like that. With a rush of wild exhilaration he had taken Kate's hand and jumped off the edge of the cliff, self-preservation blown to the wind. Totally consumed by that all-powerful, all-consuming thing called love, he'd had no choice but to obey the fierce command of his heart.

She had been beautiful, funny, clever…like no woman he had ever met before. The summer they had spent together in his home town of Agia Loukia, had been so special, so wonderful, that Nikos had assumed their joy would last for ever. And when Kate had accepted his proposal of marriage he had thought their future set, their happiness complete.

But too late Nikos had realised that when you jumped off a cliff, at some point you had to come back down to earth. And the crash landing he and Kate had made had been spectacularly horrendous.

Discovering that Kate had never told her parents about him—never even mentioned him—had been the first punch in the gut. No wonder she hadn't wanted him to accompany her to New York when her father had been taken ill. No wonder she hadn't wanted him at Bernie's funeral.

His first niggling thoughts that she might actually be *ashamed* of him had soon solidified into rock-hard certainty as Kate had continued to treat him with cold distance…holding him at arm's length, pushing him away. Gone had been the warm and loving woman he had fallen in love with in Crete, to be replaced by someone he'd barely recognised—someone who had hardly been able to bring herself to look at him.

Their final showdown had had an air of inevitability about it. But even so it had been far harder, far more painful than Nikos could ever have imagined. Discovering what Kate *really* thought of him, and the pitifully low opinion she had of him, had felt like a stab to the heart. It still did.

But now it was time to expunge that memory. Now the tables had turned. Now Nikos intended to exact his revenge.

The concierge behind the gleaming wooden desk indicated the elevator for Kandy Kate's headquarters. Not the sleek, burnished gold affair at the end of the lobby, but a much smaller one, with an old-fashioned metal grid that you had to pull across manually. There was a moment's hesitation after Nikos pressed the button, and then the elevator slowly ground its way down to what felt like the bowels of the earth.

He had decided not to announce his arrival.

He preferred to take his chances rather than give Kate the opportunity to disappear or prepare pretty lies. In his experience an element of surprise always worked in his favour.

The Kandy Kate office was at the end of a long corridor, its name stuck on the middle panel of a half-glazed door. After a single sharp knock Nikos walked straight in.

The room was small, gloomy and empty. There was no natural light, and a fluorescent strip bulb cast a depressingly cold glow over a cluttered desk, a couple of wooden chairs. A rustling noise to the left alerted him to another, smaller room, not much more than a cupboard. Someone of indeterminate age and sex was in there, squatting on the floor in front of an open filing cabinet drawer.

'Hi!' Nikos raised his voice as the person obviously hadn't heard him. 'I'm looking for Kate O'Connor.'

He saw the figure go rigid. As it slowly moved to stand Nikos felt the breath catch in his throat. *Of course.* She still hadn't turned around, but as she pulled out the buds in her ears, cutting short the tinny buzz of music from the phone she retrieved from her pocket, it was obvious. The shape of the back of her head, the long sweep of her neck…

Once again it had taken him a couple of seconds to recognise her, but if this was another disguise she was going to have to try a lot harder.

He advanced further into the room, positioning himself in the doorway of the glorified cupboard. 'I see I have found her.'

'Nikos!'

His name was a dry accusation on her tongue. As she finally turned to face him Nikos caught the alarm in her wide green eyes, saw the way her face had drained of colour. He heard the snatch of her indrawn breath. It was all suitably gratifying.

Nikos blatantly stared at her, ignoring the normal rules of decorum. They were way past that.

She was dressed entirely in black, her face free from make-up, her dark hair cropped short, cut into the nape of her neck so that it exposed her ears. With an unwanted kick of lust Nikos found himself wondering how that hair would feel beneath his fingertips. She looked elegant, fragile, beautiful. Certainly nothing like the woman he had seen last night. A pair of plain silver earrings dangling from her lobes were the only hint of adornment.

She looked away, avoiding his gaze. Nikos could see her desperately working to regain her composure, to pull a mask of indifference into place. He held the silence.

'What do you want?' Her voice sounded faint. 'Why are you here?'

'That's not much of a greeting, Kate.' Now his taunting animosity had kicked in. 'Not much of a welcome after all these years.'

'You'll get no welcome from me.' Her head swung back, her words falling like shards of glass.

'No. Of course I won't. How foolish of me.'

With a mocking stare, he stepped out of the doorway back into the office. After a moment's hesitation he strode over to a chair, picking up the pile of papers from the seat and holding them in his hand as he waited for Kate to squeeze in the other side of the desk.

'All right if I sit down?'

He waved the papers at her and Kate snatched them back. Nikos seated himself, stretching out his legs and crossing them at the ankles before linking his hands behind his head and leaning back in a classic display of dominance.

'So, tell me, Kate—how have you been?' He let his eyes drift over her face, watching the way the colour flooded back.

Kate gave him a fierce glare. 'I'm sure you haven't come here to ask after my well-being. I repeat, Nikos, what do you want?'

'A cup of coffee would be nice, since you're asking.'

'What do you mean by walking in here un-invited?' Her breath sounded dry in her throat.

'I make a habit of turning up uninvited.' Nikos gave her a pleasant smile. 'You should know that by now.' He watched as his barb sank in. 'Now, how about that coffee? Black, one sugar for me. But I expect you remember that.'

Kate hesitated, looking as if she'd rather boil her head in oil than make him a cup of coffee. But then, obviously deciding it wasn't worth the battle, she laid the papers down on the desk and moved over to a coffee maker in the corner of the room, her shoulders hitched up around her ears. As she removed the jug from the hotplate Nikos could see the way her hand tremored.

Good. He was glad of the effect he was having on her. It wasn't much consolation after the way she had treated him, but it was a start. And it all increased his sense of power.

As Kate passed the mug to him he deliberately let his hand touch hers, acknowledging the frisson between them with a quirk of dark brows before Kate jerked her hand away.

Yes, he was enjoying this.

'So, are these now the sole premises of the Kandy Kate empire?' He briefly glanced around him, his tone light and casual, but no less cutting for that.

'They are.'

Kate moved back behind the desk, reluctantly sitting down and folding her arms across her chest. She wore a black ribbed jumper with a scoop neck, the sleeves pushed up, and Nikos could see she had lost weight. But the clingy material still accentuated her shape nicely. She looked sober, chic...*sexy.*

'This office is perfectly adequate.'

'I'm sure it is.' Nikos gave a small nod of agreement. 'With the state of the Kandy Kate empire at the moment I imagine you could run it from a phone booth. After all, how much room do you need to go bankrupt?'

'Kandy Kate is *not* going bankrupt!' Kate was on her feet in a second, green eyes flashing.

'No?' Nikos tempered her fire with infuriating calm. 'Well, that's not what I've heard.'

'Well, you've heard wrong.'

She tossed her head, turning away from him, her face in profile. Nikos stared at the straight line of her nose, the fine sweep of her jaw. Why had he never noticed her jawline before? He'd thought he was all too familiar with every inch of Kate's body.

During the weeks they had spent together he had made it his mission to explore every delicious inch of her with his fingers, his lips, his tongue. Making love to Kate had been the most erotic experience of his life—a shared wonder that neither of them had been able to get enough of, as if they had both been taken over by an insatiable craving.

On reflection, he hadn't made love *to* her, he had made love *with* her. A symphony of sexual pleasures that had ruined him for any other woman.

And he cursed her for it.

He had cursed her when he'd arrived back in Crete after being all but banished from her home.

When the very thought of her name had been enough to solidify his blood. He had cursed her during the intervening years when, no matter how attractive a woman might be, how charming and how available, they'd all seemed about as sexy as a block of wood to Nikos after the intense earthly pleasures he had shared with Kate O'Connor. Even drinking himself into oblivion hadn't helped—just made his self-disgust second only to the disgust he'd felt for his ex-fiancée.

And he still cursed her now.

Nikos hadn't realised just how much until he'd gazed at her haughty profile and realised that time, far from diminishing his desire for Kate, had merely held it in cold storage, frozen, ready to be thawed by one fiery glance from those dark green eyes.

He took a mouthful of coffee, slamming the brakes on thoughts which were taking him in very unwanted directions—directions that had nothing to do with his carefully calculated plans. He needed to focus on what he was here to do.

'So, Kandy Kate's not in trouble then?' The venom in his voice was held just under the surface. 'The reports that your sales have plummeted, your suppliers are threatening legal action, your staff are not getting paid...' he leant forward, idly picking up a sheaf of papers, scanning a few lines before letting them drop '...all totally untrue?'

'Yes.' Kate pointedly straightened the papers, then held them to her chest. 'Well, wildly exaggerated anyway.' She refused to meet his eye.

'Is that right?' Nikos continued. 'So the fact that your share prices plummeted means nothing either? Your shareholders are perfectly happy to have received no dividends in the past twelve months and to have seen their investments dwindle to a pittance?'

'As a matter of fact...' she jutted out her chin '...share prices have increased considerably recently. Confidence in the brand is growing.'

'Really?' Nikos queried amiably. 'Or is it that someone is about to make a hostile takeover?'

Kate bit down on her lip, the nip against her soft pink pout stirring Nikos somewhere deep and low.

'Well, either way it's none of your concern. In fact I would like you to leave. Immediately.'

She moved the few steps to the door to usher him out but Nikos was too quick for her, barring her way with his broad shoulders and towering height.

'Well, that's just where you're wrong. It *is* my concern. Or at least it very soon will be.'

'What do you mean by that?' Kate stopped stock-still.

'I'm sure you can work it out for yourself, Kate.' Nikos smiled at her. 'You're a bright girl.'

'You...?' Her hand flew to tug at her earlobe. 'You mean it's *you* who has been buying up the shares?'

He rested his arm against the doorjamb. He wasn't going to reply. He would make her squirm while his silence spoke for him.

'But why? Why would you do such a thing?'

'Because I think Kandy Kate is an interesting proposition.' He casually slid his hand down the doorframe and into the pocket of his trousers. 'Handled correctly, I'm confident it will prove to be a good investment.'

'*"A good investment"?*' Kate challenged. 'I don't believe you. Why would you think that?'

Nikos gave a short laugh. 'No wonder your business is in such dire straits if you have so little faith in it.'

'I have plenty of faith in Kandy Kate, thank you very much. It's *you* I have no faith in.'

'Ah, yes, of course.' His eyes gleamed darkly. 'I almost forgot.'

'Well, I haven't.'

He could see that Kate was slowly clawing her way to safer ground. He would let her rest there for a while before bringing her straight back down.

'And there was me thinking you'd be *grateful* to find an investor. Even one such as myself.'

'You are *not* an investor,' Kate flew at him. 'You have gone behind my back and purchased Kandy Kate shares at a rock-bottom price with the intention of taking over the company. You said it yourself—this is a hostile takeover.'

'It doesn't *have* to be hostile.' Lowering his voice, Nikos fixed her with a glittering stare, reaching forward to take hold of her chin when she tried to turn her face away. 'In fact, if we put our minds to it, I suspect we could make it very friendly indeed.'

'In your dreams, Nikos.' Kate jerked her head away from his light grip. 'If you think I could ever be friendly with you again, in *any* capacity, then you are very much mistaken.'

Nikos watched as she tucked herself behind the safety of her desk, giving her a moment before he spoke again. 'Well, we'll see about that, won't we?' He sat back down opposite her. 'And, since you've brought up the matter of dreams, then, yes, I admit it—you have featured in mine quite largely.' He flexed his fingers to inspect his manicured nails. 'All those long, lonely nights in an empty bed, with nothing but memories to keep me company…what's a man to do…?' He looked up, spearing Kate with his gaze, registering the deep flush that had stained her cheeks, tinging the rim of her neat ears. 'Maybe it has been the same for you?'

'Get out!' On her feet again, Kate pointed to the door, her extended arm visibly shaking.

'No.' Nikos matched her stance, his voice a harsh command, all traces of teasing flirtation banished. 'I am not going anywhere, Kate. Not until you have heard what I have to say.'

'And what, exactly, do you think gives you the right to tell me what to do?'

Nikos would have liked to tell her. He could think of plenty of reasons why she should do exactly as he said. Kate O'Connor owed him—and in time he looked forward to making her see that. But not yet. If you were trying to land a wriggling fish it was best to turn the reel nice and slow.

He drew in a steadying breath. 'Let's just say it will be to your advantage.'

'I very much doubt it.' With a scoff, Kate sat back down, folding her arms tightly across her chest. 'Just say whatever it is you have to say, then get out.'

Nikos arranged his body on the chair, deliberately taking his time. Steepling his fingers, he raised his eyes to find hers. 'You may or may not know, but since we last met my fortunes have changed somewhat. I am now an extremely wealthy man.'

'So?' Kate glared at him. 'If you've just come here to brag about how rich you are, Nikos, then save your breath. I'm not interested.'

Nikos paused, taking a second to mentally erase her contemptuous remark. It was either that or teach her a lesson. And he knew exactly how he'd like to do *that*.

'Luckily for you, I am prepared to invest some of that fortune to save your business.'

'And, unluckily for you, I wouldn't accept you

as an investor if you were the last man on earth.' Her answer came back with the speed of a bullet.

'Really, Kate?' She was starting to wind him up now. 'Are you *sure* about that?'

'I said so, didn't I?'

'So what sort of man *would* you take investment from, I wonder?' Nikos narrowed his eyes, pretending to consider. 'The sort of man who might be persuaded to overlook the dire state of the business in return for other, more personal favours?'

'What are you insinuating?' Choking with outrage, Kate was on her feet again. 'How *dare* you?'

Her hand flew out to slap his face but Nikos intercepted it with ease, standing up and holding it against his chest so Kate was forced to lean her body across the desk.

'Tut-tut.' He eyeballed her. 'Violence is not the answer, Kate—you should know that.'

'Then take back what you just said!'

Her furious breath swelled her ribcage, pressing her breasts against the fine fabric of her sweater, accentuating the cleavage that Nikos found his eyes drawn to against their will.

'How dare you insinuate such a thing?'

'Because I *saw* you last night, Kate.'

He felt her hand go limp beneath his grasp, slipping away as shock rendered her silent.

She pulled back, dragging in a breath. 'You saw me?' Her skin visibly paled beneath the cruel strip light.

'Uh-huh.'

'Well, whatever it was you *thought* you saw, you were wrong. It was just a waitressing job—that's all.'

'A waitressing job that entailed squirming on the lap of that bloated banker? Assuming that you weren't doing it for your own sexual gratification, I can only conclude you were doing it for other, more practical reasons. I liked the blonde wig, by the way. Very classy.'

'I don't have to explain myself to *you*.' Kate valiantly fought to regain her dignity. 'If it gives you some sort of perverted pleasure to imagine that I would have sex with a stranger for money, then go ahead—be my guest. Frankly, your opinion of me is of no interest. You can think whatever you damn well like.'

'It doesn't give me pleasure, Kate. Quite the reverse.'

Slowly she scanned his face, and Nikos felt his

facial muscles pull taut beneath the scrutiny of that dark green gaze.

'Why, Nikos? Why does it bother you? Why would you care what I do?'

She was taunting him. Nikos cursed inwardly. His voice had been too raw, had betrayed too much emotion, exposing feelings he had fully intended to keep concealed. Far from reeling her in slowly, he was in danger of letting her off the hook.

'After all, we mean nothing to one another any more.' Kate pressed harder. 'We are free to see whoever we want, to do whatever we want.'

'And this is what you want, is it?' Anger fired through him. 'To be free to sell your body to the highest bidder? To anyone who's prepared to sling some money your way so you can prop up your pathetically failing business for a bit longer?'

He saw her swallow, her throat moving in the long column of her neck. But she kept her head held high.

'And what if it is? What's it to you?'

Nikos clamped down on his jaw, fighting to contain the hot sweep of masculine rage that threatened to consume him. He would *not* let her get to him.

Circling the desk, he stood before her, his shoulders back, his breathing heavy. Capturing her eyes, he made sure there was no way she could escape the cruel intensity of his gaze. 'To have a fiancée of mine behaving in such a blatantly wanton manner brings shame to my door. I will not allow it.'

'Aren't you forgetting something?' Kate blinked rapidly against his stare, but still she stayed defiant. 'I am not your fiancée any more. I haven't been for the past three years.'

'And that's why I am here. To put that right.'

'What?' Confusion spread across her lovely face.

'We are going to get engaged again, Kate. And this time we are going to see it through. This time we are going to be married.'

CHAPTER THREE

MARRIED? KATE STARED at him in open-mouthed astonishment. *No, she couldn't have heard right.* Her brain was obviously still reeling from the discovery that Nikos had seen her at the Executives' Club last night. Still burning from his hugely insulting accusation.

Going to slap his face had been stupid—an instinctive reaction she now regretted. But like a cornered animal she had fought back, when she should have been trying her hardest to show Nikos she didn't care what he thought of her. Even if she'd been dying inside.

But now, with his dark eyes boring into her, studying her face with brooding concentration, it was clear that Nikos was indeed waiting for an answer, forcing Kate to accept that she really had heard right. Though technically, of course, it hadn't even been a question—just a forceful statement of fact.

Well, he couldn't make her to do anything.

He had no power over her, no matter how much those hypnotic eyes and that arrogantly held posture said otherwise.

'Married!' She tried for a contemptuous laugh, but it came out more as a strangled cry. 'Are you crazy?'

'No, not crazy.' His voice was perfectly calm. 'Far from it.'

'Then why would you suggest such a ludicrous idea?' Hers was bordering on hysterical.

'Because circumstances mean that I am currently in need of a wife, and I think you would be the ideal candidate.'

Kate gazed at him in stunned disbelief.

What circumstances? And why her? And why was her heart thumping so wildly it hurt?

'Well, you can think again.' She battled against the heady power of his stare. Against everything he had ever meant to her and everything he still did. 'I have no idea why you think that I would even *consider* marrying you.'

'Then let me enlighten you.' Nikos raised his hand, selecting his little finger to emphasis his first point. 'Your company is in such dire financial straits that you would do anything to save it. Something you demonstrated last night only too clearly.' His top lip curled with distaste. 'You have no other investors, nowhere else to turn, and without my help this is the end of the road for Kandy Kate. You are an intelligent woman and you know this is your last chance. Because if you don't agree to my terms I will be taking over Kandy Kate anyway, and once it's under my control who knows what I will do with it?'

With all his fingers pulled back, one by one, he looked at his raised hand, then back again to Kate.

'Is that enough to be going on with?'

'So this is blackmail?' Kate's voice faltered with horror. 'If I don't agree to marry you you will ruin my family business—is that what you're saying?'

'Your family business is already ruined, Kate. The sooner you wise up to that, the better. Any investor—myself included—would simply strip the company of any remaining assets, then sell out to one of the major corporations. Obviously they would ditch the name, close the factories, merge what's left of the business with their own brands.'

'No!' She let out a yelp of anguish. 'I won't let that happen.'

'I thought as much.' Nikos fixed her with a steady gaze. 'Then it looks as if I am your only option.'

Kate bit down hard on her lip. Everything about his harshly determined face—the firm line of his mouth, the dark glitter in his eyes—spelled out the fact that he meant what he said. Nikos Nikoladis had both the power to save Kandy Kate and to ruin it.

Pulling her gaze away, she drew in a much-needed breath. She looked around her at the tiny cluttered office, with its low ceiling and peeling paintwork. It felt as if her life had shrunk... closed in on her. As if she was in a tunnel with no sign of light at the end. And the tunnel was now blocked by the menacing presence of her ex-lover.

'So what are these *circumstances*?' Kate tried to get the fog of her mind to clear. 'Why do you need a wife?'

It sounded even more stupid when she said it out loud. Even more archaic.

'I will explain.' Nikos glanced around her office in much the same way as she had. 'But not here. This place depresses me.'

Welcome to my world.

It depressed Kate as well—not that she would admit it to him.

She watched as he strode towards the door, stepping back to usher her through.

'Come on.' He gestured impatiently. 'I'll find us somewhere that serves a decent cup of coffee.'

Nikos's choice of venue was an old-fashioned Greek diner, tucked away up a nearby side street. Seating them in one of the booths, he ordered them both coffee without bothering to ask Kate what she wanted.

In the banquette seat opposite him, Kate had to wait for the waitress to bring their order before she could start her interrogation.

'So, what's this all about?'

She plunged right in, anxious to get this ordeal over with as quickly as possible. The sooner Nikos told her what he wanted from her, the sooner she could inform him that it wasn't going to happen and he could disappear from her life again.

Nikos took a sip of coffee, slowly replacing the cup to its saucer. 'You remember Philippos?'

The question was as direct as it was surprising.

'Yes, of course.' Kate replied quickly. 'Your friend in Agia Loukia.'

'He died.' His voice was cold, unemotional. 'Two months ago.'

'Oh!' Kate's hand went to her chest. 'I'm very sorry to hear that.'

Nikos shrugged as if her sympathy was of no consequence.

'What happened?'

'An accidental overdose.' Nikos continued matter-of-factly. 'He was self-medicating while the balance of his mind was disturbed.'

'I'm *so* sorry,' Kate repeated, recalling the awkward young man Nikos had introduced her to during that summer in Crete, describing the reluctant individual as his 'genius new business partner'.

Kate remembered how Philippos hadn't been able to meet her eye, instead flashing a panicked look at Nikos because he might have to interact with this alien female creature.

'I know what good friends you were,' she said.

'He was a good friend of mine, certainly, but I'm not sure the same could be said of my friendship with him.' Nikos looked away.

Kate stared at his profile in surprise.

'Anyway...' He turned his head back, the shutters coming down to conceal that chink of vulnerability. 'Philippos has a younger sister—Sofia.'

'Yes, I remember.' Kate thought back. 'She would be how old now? Fourteen? Fifteen?'

'She's fifteen.'

'This must be so terribly sad for her. Didn't you say that their parents died in a road accident some time ago?'

Nikos nodded.

'So she's all alone in the world. Poor Sofia.'

'One thing she is *not* is poor. When she comes of age she will inherit Philippos's largely untouched fortune.'

'I didn't mean that sort of poor. I meant—'

'I know what you meant.' Bluntly interrupting her, Nikos folded his arms across his chest. 'But because of her wealth Sofia needs protecting. There are people out there already making moves to try and get their hands on her money.'

'She must be grieving so badly I don't suppose she cares about that now.'

'She might not care, but I do.' His shoulders stiffened. 'Which is why I have applied to the courts to become her legal guardian.'

'Her *guardian*?' Kate couldn't hide her astonishment. She had already seen Nikos undergo one transformation, from laid-back lover to hotshot businessman. But this was not a role she would ever have put him down for. 'But what do *you* know about raising a teenage girl?

'That is none of your concern.' Nikos brutally cut her short. 'The important thing is I will be able to protect her fortune, invest it wisely for her, until she is old enough to know what she wants to do with it.'

Kate looked down, tracing the grains of sugar on the tabletop with her finger as she imagined how Sofia must be feeling. She had never met the teenager, the summer she had been in Agia Loukia—Sofia had been away on some sort of exchange scheme if Kate remembered correctly. But even so her heart went out to her.

Kate's own family was far from perfect, but at least she still had a mother. Did Sofia really have no one to care for her?

'Surely the most important thing is to find her a secure home?' She faced Nikos again. 'Somewhere that she feels safe…loved. Where all her emotional needs will be met.'

'Then I will do that too.' Fierce determination lit Niko's eyes. 'But let me make one thing clear, Kate: I am *not* here to seek your opinion on child welfare. Your role in this is quite straightforward.'

He pushed his coffee cup decisively to one side.

'It is a condition of the courts that in order to become Sofia's guardian I have to prove I am in a stable relationship—preferably married.'

He paused, gauging the way the penny was dropping. And drop it did—clattering through Kate like a cold weight.

'What I need now is an agreement from you that you will be my wife.'

Kate blinked, reminding herself to breathe. This was the second time Nikos had proposed to her, but the circumstances couldn't be more different. The first time had been such a tender, joyful experience. They had been so much in love, and Kate had been convinced their happiness would last for ever. How wrong she had been.

And now this. A cold, calculated business deal, delivered by a man with no emotion. No heart. Kate closed her eyes against the pain that suddenly lanced through her. Pain she had told herself she no longer felt. She had been wrong about that too.

She opened her eyes again to see Nikos staring at her, waiting for an answer. From the firm set of his jaw she could see how important this was to him, and the cold, steely determination in his eyes left no room for doubt.

But no... *No!* The whole idea was sheer madness. She needed to end this now.

'My answer is no, Nikos.' She shook her head for emphasis, desperately trying to ignore the thud of her heart. She could see Nikos's features hardening as she spoke. 'I can't do it. It wouldn't be right.'

'And to see Sofia delivered into the hands of a distant relative—a great-uncle whom she has never met, who has only come crawling out of the woodwork now because of Sofia's fortune, who doesn't give a damn about her or Philippos for that matter—that *would* be right, would it?'

Nikos's reply was hot and harsh, and anger flared his nostrils. The strength of his conviction was unmistakable, and his tautly held frame, the fierce glare in his eyes, were all saying one thing. He was serious about this. *Deadly* serious.

'But there must be someone else who could

act as her guardian. Some other relative—or a family friend, maybe?' Kate raised her brows hopefully.

'There is no one else. I am the only person to have Sofia's best interests at heart. I know this is what Philippos would have wanted.'

'But he didn't name you as her guardian in his will?'

'There *is* no will. Philippos never made one.'

This didn't surprise Kate. She hadn't known him well, but Philippos had struck her as the kind of guy who struggled with the practicalities of life. His brilliant mind had been able to conjure up amazing new ways to revolutionise the software industry, but somehow his shoelaces would always come undone.

'Why me?' She pulled nervously at her earlobe again. From the storm of questions still buzzing around her head it was the first one to form on her lips. 'Why do you want me to marry you when no doubt there is a host of beautiful, eligible women who would be only too happy to be your bride.'

'I'm flattered you think me such a catch.' Nikos gave her a complacent smile. 'But the fact is it's you that I want.'

A surge of ridiculous optimism bloomed inside Kate, appearing from nowhere and spreading hot and fast to every part of her body. Was it possible that Nikos still had feelings for her? That he might want to try and make amends? To win her back?

She slammed the brakes on her ridiculously wayward thoughts. It was terrifying the way Nikos could make her feel…the power he still had over her.

'But *why*?' She repeated the question, fighting to keep herself grounded.

'Because I know how desperate you are.'

Ha! If Kate had needed a shot of realism there it was, delivered with unerring accuracy, straight to the heart. She felt herself crumple inside, that foolish hope creeping back to wherever it had come from. How had she even let that happen? Had she not learned her lesson? Had the intervening years taught her *nothing*?

She sat up straighter, steeling herself to meet his gaze. 'I may be desperate.' Somehow she managed to hold her voice steady. 'But I'm not *that* desperate.'

'No?' His reply was immediate. 'Are you sure about that, Kate?'

'Quite sure.'

Silence fell between them, punctuated only by the sound of Nikos's fingers drumming lightly on the table.

'Look, just consider the facts.'

Kate could hear the effort it was taking him to make himself sound reasonable.

'You need money. I need a wife. You would be foolish to make any decision until you've heard my proposal.'

'Not as foolish as I would be to consider getting involved with *you* again. In any capacity.' The painful memories were a useful tool to stop her bravado from slipping. 'My decision is made, Nikos.'

'Well, it's the wrong one!'

Nikos's paper-thin patience was ripped apart. A tell-tale muscle ticked in his cheek as he drew in a sharp breath, clenching his hands on the table before him.

'Think about it, Kate.' He'd reined in his temper, but his knuckles were pulled white. 'This arrangement will suit us both. You agree to be my wife until the court rule in my favour and I get legal custody of Sofia. In return I will save Kandy Kate. I will provide whatever funds are necessary to pay off your creditors, get the business thriving again. We are talking about pretty much a blank cheque here, Kate. Imagine what you could do with that...'

Kate imagined. A large injection of money was exactly what Kandy Kate needed. Once the business was stable again she was confident she would be able make a success of it. It was like being in the bottom of a pit—she just needed a boost to get out, then she could run.

'And, of course, you will have the benefit of my business knowledge and my contacts—many of whom are extremely influential. There is no reason why you shouldn't massively expand Kandy Kate...grow the business as big as you want.' Nikos pressed on relentlessly.

Kate closed her ears. She mustn't let herself be seduced by this daydream.

'No, Nikos—'

She started to speak but just then the waitress reappeared to refill their cups, so she paused, watching the way the young woman hovered around Nikos's side as if she couldn't quite bring herself to leave. When Nikos looked up to thank her, a pretty flush spread to her cheeks.

'Then do it for Sofia.' When the waitress finally moved away Nikos jumped in, cutting Kate off before she could speak. 'Think about *her*.'

'I… I am thinking about Sofia.' Kate's heart twisted. 'I genuinely feel very sorry for her.'

'Then do something about it—feeling sorry is not enough.' The full glare of his attention was on her now. 'Marry me and you will help secure her future. Walk away and that greedy, manipulative uncle of hers may well be granted legal guardianship.'

'I don't know…' Kate took in a panicked breath. 'I mean, just supposing we were to marry, and the courts did award you guardianship of Sofia, what then?'

'Then we divorce. Sofia will be legally protected, and you will have resurrected your business. It's the obvious solution.'

Kate swallowed. Nikos made it sound so practical, so easy. Perhaps it was. She didn't doubt that if she turned him down Nikos would find someone else to do his bidding. That small interaction with the waitress had proved the power he had over women. If she didn't do this someone else would benefit from the money she needed so desperately to save Kandy Kate.

'But what about Sofia? Won't she be expecting us to be a proper married couple? How will she feel if we divorce as soon as she's legally your care?'

'You will leave Sofia to me.' Nikos's tone left no room for discussion. 'Your role is to help me secure guardianship. Nothing more.'

A heavy silence fell between them, and the hiss of the coffee machine, the babble of voices in the diner, faded away into the background as Kate found herself staring into the mesmerising deep brown eyes of this all-powerful man.

'So what do you say…?' His voice had lowered, become dark, seductive, compelling.

Taking in a gasp of air, Kate forced herself to break his gaze, looking around her for some sort of respite from the intense focus that was making it so impossible to think straight. But her brain was blocked by the man in front of her, by what he was offering her—the dream of being able save Kandy Kate was hanging there, tantalisingly within reach.

When Nikos reached for her hand, lying on the table between them, his touch jolted through her like an electric shock, whipping her gaze back to his face. Once again she was caught.

'Do we have a deal?'

And from somewhere deep inside her, a hidden part that should never even have had a voice, she heard words bubbling up inside her. Before she knew it they were on her lips, spoken.

'Okay.' She held her breath. 'I'll do it.'

Nikos exhaled with satisfaction. And not a little relief. *He'd got her.* The minor triumph felt good.

For all his outward confidence, and his brusque, businesslike assertiveness that Kate would accept his offer as the only sensible course of action—snatch his hand off, in fact—deep down he'd been none too sure how she'd react.

Kate O'Connor was a law unto herself, and after the way they had parted anything could have happened. But he'd done it. Now he just had to close the deal.

He leant back in the booth, his arms behind his head as he surveyed the space where Kate had sat before excusing herself to go to the bathroom. She hadn't been able to get out fast enough, sliding across the seat and straightening those long legs before disappearing into the depths of the diner behind him. If she was regretting her decision, trying to think her way out of it, it was too late. She had already sealed her fate.

Nikos took another mouthful of coffee. The reason why he had been so insistent that Kate and only Kate must be the woman he would take for his wife he preferred not to examine in too much depth. All he knew was that as soon as his lawyers had told him his case for guardianship would be considerably strengthened if he was married Kate's name had come into his head. And once there it had refused to shift.

He'd spent so long trying to erase her from his mind, trying to rid himself of her memory, rueing the day he had ever met her, it had almost become an obsession. But he was forced to admit that where Kate was concerned obsession came all too easily. His mistake had been confusing it for love.

Infatuation had been there from the start. Coming across her that evening, seated at one of the rickety tables on the beach outside his father's *taverna*, Nikos had been instantly smitten. With her long dark hair and gorgeous eyes, the dazzling smile she had given him when she had taken the menu out of his hands had arrowed straight to his heart—or his groin...or both. Making it his mission to find out everything about her, he had quickly discovered that she was on a solo three-month tour of Europe and that her first stop had been Athens, where someone had recommended this 'wonderful little place' in Crete and here she was.

What she had failed to mention was that she was part of an extremely wealthy American confectionery dynasty that actually bore her name.

Captivated by her exotic American beauty, her New York accent, her enthusiastic and infectious love of all things Cretan, Nikos had been guilty of seriously neglecting the other diners that night—until he had been pulled back into line by his father, Marios, fiery chef and owner of the modest establishment, who had stood on the terrace with his hands on his hips, demanding that Nikos stopped flirting with the customers and did some 'goddamn work'.

The relationship between Nikos and his father had never been an easy one. Left to raise Nikos on his own, after Nikos's mother had upped and left them when Nikos was still a toddler, Marios had struggled to be the parent he should have been. He had resorted to the bottle more than had been good for him, or Nikos, and there had been far too many drunken rages, far too many times when Marios had blamed Nikos for his wife walking out on them, for not being a good enough son either then or now.

For ruining his life.

Marios would regret it when he sobered up, but even then somehow he had never been able to find the words to apologise, instead preferring to show his remorse with a plate of food, which he would gruffly set down in front of his son, ruffling Nikos's dark curls when he was a boy, slapping him on the back as a young man.

Nikos had never blamed his father—maybe he was right…maybe it *was* his fault that his mother had walked out on them both—but Marios's mood swings had meant that Nikos had decided he was going to leave home as soon as possible, reasoning that his *papa* would be better off without him.

Aged sixteen he had moved to Athens, picking up any job he could to keep himself off the streets. At eighteen he'd managed to get a scholarship to university, followed by a year's national service in the army. With a taste for adventure he had then travelled around Europe for several months, with no plans to stop, until an impassioned plea from his father, insisting that his health was failing and that he needed his son to help him run the *taverna*, had brought Nikos back to his home village of Agia Loukia.

As it had turned out, Marios's 'failing health' had been a scam. The old man had been fine—better than ever, in fact, as he had finally laid off the ouzo. Nikos had seen straight through his father's ruse to get him to move back home permanently. And he'd certainly had no intention of 'paying a visit' to Agnes Demopoulous's youngest daughter Ilena, either, pretty as she was.

Nikos had recognised a trap when he'd seen one. Besides, he'd had no intention of finding a wife and settling down. Far from it. That road led only to misery. One summer—that was all he'd promised his father. Then he would be out of there.

But a lot could change in one summer…

The first trigger had been meeting up again with his old school friend, Philippos. Nikos had already heard the tragic news that Philippos's parents had been killed in a car crash a couple of years ago, leaving him and his little sister to fend for themselves. Keen to see if he could be of any help while he was in Agia Loukia, Nikos had sat himself down at Philippos's table expecting nothing more than a cup of coffee in return for his offer of help.

But when Philippos had started talking about the project he was working on—how he'd found a way to print circuits onto flexible plastic—Nikos had instantly seen the potential. He'd known it could be big—huge! Something that Philippos's brilliant but totally non-businesslike brain hadn't even considered.

Promising that this was going to make their fortune, Nikos had formed a joint business with him and set about doing just that. At that point neither of them had had two cents to their names, which had meant securing investment was difficult. But with boundless enthusiasm and determination Nikos had known he was going to make it work.

And then one night a remarkable woman had turned up at the *taverna*, just in time to share his adventure. Suddenly Nikos had been able to see a future, a wife, kids, the complete package. Suddenly the whole marriage thing had made sense. Here was the woman he wanted to spend the rest of his life with. Kate O'Connor—The One.

Boy, had he got *that* wrong.

Returning from the bathroom, Kate slid into

the booth opposite him again, looking slightly more composed than when she had left. Nikos acknowledged her presence with a quick quirk of a dark brow, his eyes slowly moving across her face, taking in the pursed set of her mouth, the wariness in those deep green eyes. She was nervous. Maybe she had good reason to be.

He hadn't fully decided how he was going to proceed from here, but he did know he intended to use the situation to its full advantage. He was marrying for a legitimate reason—to secure the guardianship of Sofia. But that didn't mean there wouldn't be other benefits along the way.

Revenge was an ugly word, but it was still uppermost in Nikos's mind. He and Kate had unfinished business and here was the perfect chance to put that right. He was going to make her pay for the way she had treated him. And he would enjoy doing it. He'd have to be careful he didn't enjoy it too much.

'Drink up.' Breaking the silence, he indicated the second untouched cup of coffee in front of Kate with a wave of his hand. 'If we hurry we can get a marriage license straight away.'

CHAPTER FOUR

TWENTY-FOUR HOURS LATER Kate was in a taxi, drawing up outside City Hall.

She could see Nikos on the steps of the building even before the cab slowed to a halt. Amid the sea of people his tall, dark figure was unmissable, standing alone, arms behind his back, his eyes scanning the traffic.

Waiting for her.

Paying the driver, Kate felt her last bit of independence slipping away with the coins she dropped into his hand. She had flatly refused Nikos's offer of a limousine to pick her up, insisting that she would find her own way, thank you very much. This whole wedding was enough of a farce as it was, without adding insult to injury with fancy cars and pointless traditions.

Snapping her purse shut, she stood on the pavement, knowing without looking round that Nikos had seen her, that he was coming down the steps to greet her. There was no escape.

Taking a deep breath, she smoothed down the fabric of her dress. *This was it, then.* A couple of days ago Nikos had been firmly part of her past, blocked out as best she could, the misery locked away, buried deep within her. If anyone had told her she would be marrying the man who had hurt her so badly—and so astonishingly quickly—she would have thought they were completely insane.

And yet here she was, about to do just that. About to tie herself to Nikos Nikoladis for the foreseeable future.

She started up the steps, one at a time, concentrating on the bright red high-heeled shoes she had put on today in the hope of giving herself a bit of much-needed confidence. The short white lace dress she had had for years, but it fitted the bill well enough. She'd hardly had time to buy a new outfit even if she'd wanted to, which she hadn't.

To her horror, Nikos had insisted that they marry right away, brushing aside Kate's objections and maintaining that delaying matters wasn't going to help either of them. When Kate had finally conceded that he might have a point she had been rushed off to secure a marriage license there and then.

In a complete daze she had found herself at the clerk's office, providing identification, signing forms, committing to this mad idea before she'd had any chance to think it through. She was sure if Nikos could have found a way to circumnavigate the rule that said they had to wait twenty-four hours between getting the license and getting wed they would have been married on the spot. But it seemed that was beyond even *his* powers of persuasion, so reluctantly he had arranged to meet her here precisely one day later.

'You look beautiful.'

Suddenly he was in front of her, all around her, filling her vision, her senses, blotting out everything else. He smelled divine. When he took her elbow she had no choice but to look at him, at the immaculately cut dark suit, the shirt collar glowing white against his olive skin, the blue silk tie perfectly knotted. As her gaze was pulled to his handsome face she met the glitter in his eyes, the slight smile that lightly curved his sensuous lips. The sort of smile a fox might give a chicken.

Kate fought against the fierce kick of desire just the sight of him produced. So dark and suave, so drop-dead gorgeous, he was the epitome of the perfect groom. On the outside, at least. Inside was a different matter.

In a complete turnaround, Kate had to keep reminding herself of the way he had treated her, after spending the last three years desperately trying to block it out. If she was to stand any chance of combatting the tumultuous surge of emotions he stirred in her with little more than a glance from those deep brown eyes she *had* to focus on the man he really was. On what he was capable of.

'Here.' Nikos produced a bunch of flowers from behind his back. 'I thought the bride should have a bouquet.'

Kate took the flowers from his outstretched hand. A mixture of blood-red peonies and soft pink roses. They were beautiful, of course. Nikos had always had impeccable taste. But to Kate the bouquet felt like a symbol of his possession, and his deliberate use of the word 'bride' had underlined the role she had to play.

She drew in another breath. No one was forcing her to marry Nikos. This was *her* decision.

That was something she had been silently repeating like a mantra this past twenty-four hours. Through a sleepless night when the twisted bedsheets had seemed to rise up to strangle her, into the harsh light of a new day, glaring like a cruel spotlight on her many misgivings.

Long term, this was the sensible decision—even if it no longer felt like it. She was helping Sofia and she was saving Kandy Kate. And she was in way too deep to pull out now.

Clutching the flowers to her chest, she let Nikos take her arm, tucking it through his as he started to move them up the steps towards the register office. He was holding her closely to him in an outward show of affection, the way a loving groom about to get married should behave. But they were no loving couple, and Nikos's firm touch only made her skin skitter with nerves.

Nerves that increased tenfold as Kate sat on the bench awaiting their turn, her bouquet lying in her lap, watching the other couples coming and going.

They all appeared so happy, so much in love, and it twisted her heart with pain. In contrast, her own groom was pacing up and down like a caged lion, glancing at his watch as if time was of the utmost importance, then looking back at her as if to check she was still there, grim determination written all over his face.

Finally their number was called, and together they walked into the clerk's office. With rapid efficiency, the officiant ran through the legalities, the marriage certificate was signed by themselves and two witnesses who had been procured for the purpose, and that was it—they were married!

The whole thing felt like a dream to Kate—some sort of confused fantasy that she would wake from at any moment. But as they walked out into the fresh air, the sunlight flashing on the gold band on her finger, Kate knew this was no illusion. She was now legally married to Nikos Nikoladis, and somehow she was going to have to work out a way to deal with it.

Somehow, over the next few months, she had to find a way to protect herself from this man, from the brutal effect he had on her heart. From all that Nikos was and all that he had meant to her. If she didn't she knew he had the power to crush her yet again. She was sure of it.

'Hey, Kandy Kate!'

A paparazzi photographer appeared from nowhere, making Kate jump. This was all she needed. She hated the paps, having been at their mercy her entire life. Instinctively she turned to-wards Nikos for protection.

'Hold it right there for me, baby—that's it. Can you turn this way? Beautiful!'

Why wasn't Nikos telling this guy where to go?

Kate looked up at him, her beseeching eyes making it obvious that she needed help—needed Nikos to tell this chancer to clear off. She'd tell him herself, but she was didn't want to draw any more attention to herself than was absolutely necessary. People were already turning to stare. The Kandy Kate name was enough to stop them in their tracks, see them pulling out their cell phones.

But, to her horror, Nikos showed no sign of warning off the photographer—quite the reverse. Pulling her tightly by his side, he moved them so that the guy could get the most advantageous shot. With the camera shutter clicking away fu-riously, not to mention the small crowd that had gathered around them, taking pictures on their phones, they were causing quite a stir.

'Nikos!' With a panicky intake of breath, Kate hissed at him. '*Do* something.'

'I *am* doing something.' Bringing his arm up

so that it wrapped around her shoulder, Nikos drew her even closer to him, giving her an affectionate squeeze. 'I'm showing off my new bride. You're the one who needs to do something— loosen up a bit. Make this look believable.'

'Hey, Kate, over here!'

Another photographer had arrived, pounding up the steps and elbowing his way through the crowd, a battery of cameras bouncing against his chest.

'Congratulations, guys!' Holding a camera high, he adjusted the massive lens. 'How about a nice big smile?'

'Oh, I think we can do better than that.'

With no warning Nikos took Kate's face in his hands and lowered his head, covering her mouth with his own in one smooth movement.

Kate gave a silent gasp, the touch of his lips momentarily paralysing her, until the heat from his mouth made sensation flood back, swelling her lips, heating them beneath his silky soft touch. For a second they stayed like that…joined, melded. Kate was unable to pull away, no matter how much she knew she should. It was all she could do to stop herself from deepening the kiss, from leaning into him and begging for more.

And all the time those camera shutters clicked noisily.

'Much better, *agape mou.*' Finally Nikos released her, his breath a soft caress against her cheek as he turned to whisper in her ear. '*So* much better. For a moment there you almost had me fooled.'

Kate pulled away, her heart thudding, shock stealing away the sharp retort his taunting comment deserved. Instead she found herself pressing her fingers to her lips as if to check that they were still intact. That they hadn't somehow been flayed by the heat of Nikos's kiss.

'Okay, guys, if you will let us through...'

Taking charge at last, Nikos moved them through the crowd, one arm outstretched to allow Kate to descend the steps beside him, the other wrapped around her waist as he fended off congratulations and questions with pleasant thanks and nods of acknowledgment.

A sleek limousine had magically drawn up alongside the kerb. As the driver opened the door Kate hurried to get inside, her heart still hammering against her ribs. Nikos slid in beside her, and as the car door shut peace descended.

Throwing the bouquet down between them, Kate drew in a furious breath.

'Well, thanks for nothing!' She turned on him as the car smoothly joined the flow of traffic. 'After that little scene we're going to be splashed all over the papers tomorrow.'

'Exactly.' Nikos's arrogant expression said it all. 'The perfect photo opportunity.'

'What?' Suddenly the light dawned, bright and sharp. 'You mean you set that up?'

Nikos shrugged. 'I happened to mention to someone I know in the newspaper business that we were getting married here today. They must have tipped off one of the photographers they use.'

He couldn't even be bothered to look at her. Instead he was tapping something into his cell phone.

'And you didn't have the decency to ask me first if it was okay?' Kate hissed back at him.

'I didn't want to spoil the surprise.'

Nikos's silky tone stole over her like a tide of prickly heat. The phone, now finished with, was slipped back into his pocket and his focus moved back to her. Which was a whole lot worse.

His slow gaze swept over her exposed thighs,

taking in the way her dress had ridden up when she'd twisted round to confront him. Furiously Kate tugged it down, lifting her bottom off the seat to try and release more of the lacy fabric. This dress was way too short. Whatever had she been thinking?

A glance in Nikos's direction revealed *his* thoughts all too clearly. The dark, very masculine gleam in his eyes was unmistakable, deeply sexual, and hot enough to scorch her soul. And the smug expression on his face told Kate he was loving every minute of her turmoil. This was a power game he was playing—displaying his obvious interest and enjoying her confused reaction to the full.

Moving her eyes to the front, Kate primly crossed her legs, feeling Nikos's stare burn a trail down her calf to her ankle and the red stiletto dangling from her foot. *Damn him.*

'Well, I did *not* appreciate the surprise. You had absolutely no right to tell the press about our wedding without asking my permission first.'

'No right, eh?'

She heard the rustle of Nikos folding his arms across his immaculately tailored chest.

'Actually, that's where you're wrong. Because

by agreeing to marry me you have also agreed to the terms of our relationship.'

'What terms?' Alarm caught in her throat as she snapped her head round to face him again. 'I didn't agree to any *terms*.'

'I think you'll find that you did.'

'Our marriage is a purely practical arrangement, entered into for our mutual benefit. I did it solely for the money, Nikos, you know that. Nothing else.'

'Ah, Kate…'

Nikos raised a hand, delicately stroking her jawline with a lover's caress. Kate's breath stalled.

'You are *such* a romantic.' His voice was heavy with sarcasm, but with seduction too, and his Greek accent, which usually gave no more than a hint of his European roots, seemed deliberately deepened to a sexy burr. 'Whatever am I going to do with you?'

'Nothing.' Kate jerked her head back to dislodge his fingers and their velvet touch. 'You are not going to do anything with me—that's the point. Whatever you may think, marrying me has *not* given you the right to take over my life.'

'Let's get a couple of things straight, shall we?'

His tone hardened as he placed his hands down on his arrogantly spread muscled thighs.

Kate remembered those hands well. Not immaculately manicured, as they were now, but roughened by his work on the fishing boats, by scrubbing tables and shucking oysters for the diners at Marios's restaurant.

On the night they had met he had presented her with a plate of oysters sitting on a bed of ice, symmetrically arranged around half a lemon. She hadn't ordered them. She had tried oysters before and decided they weren't for her. But with Nikos standing there expectantly, waiting for her to taste them, she hadn't been able to say no.

Picking up the first shell to examine it, she had been acutely aware of him watching her. And when she'd tipped back her head, letting the oyster slide down her throat, it had suddenly felt like the most erotic experience of her life.

Their eyes had met afterwards, their shared intimacy thrumming in the warm night air. Kate could still remember that moment…still taste the sea on her lips. By the end of the evening those hands had taken her to unknown heights of ecstasy.

Nikos's ruthless voice cut through the heat of her memory.

'Our lives are going to be inextricably linked for the next few months. So you had better get used to it. I need to generate publicity around our marriage to strengthen my custody application. The courts will want to see evidence of the two of us together to prove this is legitimate. Looking like we're in love.' He fixed her with a loaded stare. 'I trust that won't be a problem?'

Kate swallowed hard. No, it wasn't a problem. *It was living nightmare.*

'I will do whatever needs to be done.' She forced herself to agree. To ignore the buzz in her head that was telling her to stop the car, to get out now, to run as far away from the dangerous man as was possible to do. 'Within reason.'

'Excellent.' Nikos gave a brisk, satisfied nod. 'And this will benefit you too. All good publicity for Kandy Kate.'

'Kandy Kate is *my* affair.' Kate struggled against his commanding authority. 'I don't need your advice on how to run my business.'

'You sure about that?' Nikos taunted. 'Someone needs to do *something*. As a major investor, I would hate to see my money go straight down the pan. The first payment has already gone into your account, by the way.' He tapped the phone in his pocket. 'And the shares I own will be transferred back to you.'

'Oh, thanks…' Kate mumbled her graceless gratitude.

'But it's going to take more than just money to make Kandy Kate a success again. We need to radically alter the public's perception of the business. Replace its tawdry image with something far more cheerful…wholesome. And what better start than a sunny photo of you on the steps of City Hall, having just married the man of your dreams?'

Kate shot him a furious glance. He was loving this. And what was all this *we*?

'The man of my dreams?' She knew she shouldn't retaliate, that he was deliberately goading her, but she had to do something to try and wipe that smug look off his finely honed face. 'I don't think so, Nikos.'

'No?' Nikos gave her a sceptical glance. 'I've already admitted that you've crept into my dreams in the small hours of the night. Are you telling me it hasn't been the same for you?'

'I'm admitting nothing.'

With heat scoring her cheeks, Kate turned away, realising that by not denying it she had as good as owned up to the truth. Of *course* he had filled her dreams, dominated her thoughts—both day *and* night, for that matter—for the last three whole years. And, judging by his supercilious expression, he knew that only too well.

She stared out of the window at the New York traffic, at people going about their everyday lives, rushing around, all so busy, completely oblivious to her miserable plight. To the fact that she had just sold her soul to the devil.

'Anyway.' Nikos pulled the conversation back into line. 'Those shots will generate a buzz about the wedding in the press, and that's good publicity for us both. This is the way it's going to be from now on, Kate, so you had better get used to it.'

He had this all worked out, didn't he? Kate could feel his eyes on her profile, his gaze prickling the outline of her ear, the skin on her neck. With a trembling lip she felt the irony of her situation hit home. Once again she'd found herself being manipulated in the name of Kandy Kate. Only this time it wasn't her mother controlling her. This time it was Nikos Nikoladis. And that was a far more terrifying prospect.

'Where are we going, anyway?'

Turning back to face him, Kate swallowed down her sorrow. There was no point regretting anything now. It was done. Besides, it was a genuine question. For the first time it occurred to her that she had no idea where this purring limo was taking them.

'What do newlyweds usually do after they get married?' Nikos gave her a roguish smile.

Kate's heart rate spiked dramatically, panic strangling her vocal cords. 'Wh…what do you mean?'

'Relax, *pethi mou*.' With a low laugh, Nikos took her hand from where it had flown to the base of her throat. Holding it in his own, he turned the circle of gold on her finger. 'Not that. Unless you're offering, of course. In which case it would be rude to turn you down.'

'I am not offering anything.'

'Hmm…pity. Well, in that case I suggest you sit back and enjoy the ride. Because you and I, Mrs Kate O'Connor-Nikoladis, are about to go on honeymoon.'

CHAPTER FIVE

PARIS. KATE GAZED wistfully at the city spread out before her. The city of love. The ultimate destination for a romantic honeymoon.

She had always longed to visit Paris. That fateful summer when she had set off on her European tour it had been one of her must-see destinations. But she had never made it. Circumstances had overtaken her—Nikos had happened.

Back then, if someone had told her she would be here now, married to Nikos, honeymooning in one of the most beautiful cities in the world, she would have thought it was the fairy tale ending. The start of her happy-ever-after.

Now it felt like a mockery—a travesty. As if they were disrespecting the institution of marriage and insulting the city with their bogus relationship. Despoiling the streets for the real lovers who walked innocently hand in hand, soaking up the atmosphere.

They had been here for four days, every minute of which had been choreographed by Nikos with military precision. The Eiffel Tower—*tick*. Notre Dame—*tick*. The Louvre, the Arc de Triomphe—*tick, tick*. Their days had been a whirlwind of sightseeing, a blur of art and architecture and history, all captured by the paparazzi in carefully orchestrated photo opportunities.

Just to add to the mockery, the boutique hotel they were staying in was called L'Hôtel d'Amour. Considering the whole time they'd been here she and Nikos had scarcely spent five minutes alone together, they should have been thrown out as imposters. After days of seeing the sights, their evenings were spent dining with business acquaintances of Nikos. And as for the nights... Those were very firmly spent apart.

Their artfully designed rooms on the top floor might be side by side, but they might as well be a million miles apart. And when they stood outside their respective doors at the end of the evening they didn't exchange so much as a peck on the cheek.

It upset Kate far more than it should have. Nikos's demeanour was polite but cool, his attitude perfectly civil but businesslike. So why did it feel like salt poured into an open wound?

His flirtatious goading back in New York had wound her up tighter than a sprung coil, made the blood thunder through her veins, made her want to slap his arrogant face—hard. But it had also made her feel *alive*.

Somehow this stiff, sterile politeness was far worse. His total lack of interest in her was sapping her confidence, curling her heart into a prickly ball.

Turning away from the window, she reluctantly started to get ready for another dinner date. Tonight, apparently, they were going to the famous Moulin Rouge to watch a cabaret show. It should be fun—the perfect antidote to all the culture she had been force-fed these past few days. But the thought of spending another evening with a group of overweight businessmen, with the cold, looming spectre of Nikos across the other side of the table, watching her every move, filled her with dread.

Nikos had insisted that these endless meals in fancy restaurants were for her own benefit—or at least for the benefit of Kandy Kate. That these men—and they were *all* men —were highly influential, some of them with contacts in the confectionery trade. If Kandy Kate was to stand any chance of breaking into the European market these were the kind of people who could make it happen.

Kate hadn't bothered to argue. Up until then she had never even considered the European market. Kandy Kate had always been an all-American brand. But maybe Nikos was right—maybe she should be looking further afield. It wouldn't hurt to explore the idea. Now she had Nikos's investment behind her she could start to think big. And besides, sharing a table with noisy French businessmen had to be better than the forced intimacy of a table for two with Nikos.

Though how those guys ever actually got any business done, in between their long lunches and even longer dinners, and the copious amounts of red wine they consumed, followed by the cigars and the brandy, was a mystery to Kate. Most of them were around the same age as her father—her hardworking, virtually teetotal father—who had always watched his diet, kept fit. It didn't seem fair that they were still here when he was dead.

But then life wasn't fair. Kate was learning that pretty fast.

With a heavy sigh, she flipped through the

dresses she had brought with her, deciding which one to wear. Most of them had been bought years ago. when she'd been able to afford such luxuries, but they still served the purpose. She selected a dark red cocktail dress. One of her favourites, it was worn off the shoulder, with a fitted waist and a knee-length full skirt that twirled out when she spun around.

Not that Kate was planning on doing any twirling this evening. She would leave that strictly to the dancers. There was no frivolity to be had for *her*. She knew the form by now. Tonight was going to be another torturous evening, playing the part of Nikos's new wife with a frozen smile and an aching heart, with any attempts on her part to talk business dismissed by the other diners, who would joke that she shouldn't be concerning herself with work at a time like this.

It made a mockery of Nikos's insistence that these were useful contacts, but frankly she was past caring.

Four days into this marriage, Kate was far more worried about how she was going to manage four weeks…four months…possibly even longer…being shackled to this formidable man. According to Nikos, the custody proceedings for Sofia were already well underway and it was now a question of doing everything they could to support the application while waiting for the courts to make their decision.

Though how long that would take was anybody's guess. Kate couldn't bring herself to look any further than one day at a time. She wasn't sure her paper-thin defences or her poor fragile heart could take it.

Nikos leant back in his chair, folding his arms over his chest, having no desire to join in with the clapping, cheering audience. On the stage a group of young women were frenetically dancing, lifting their frilly red, white and blue skirts, kicking their legs unfeasibly high, baring their bottoms and doing the splits, much to the delight of the whooping crowd.

They were doing a job, he supposed, the same as the rest of them, but their efforts left him cold. As the music started to speed up even more, the noise becoming ever louder, he started to wonder how much more of this interminable show he could take.

He glanced across at Kate. She looked stunning this evening. But then she always did. When she had opened the door of her hotel room to him earlier that evening, her shoulders bare, her body held unnaturally straight, he had had to stop himself from crossing the threshold, taking her in his arms and kissing away all that pent-up tension with the soft, damp heat of his mouth. Then walking her backwards towards the bed, lifting up the full skirt and ravishing her there and then.

It had been an infinitely more attractive prospect than spending an evening watching this rowdy cabaret. It still was.

Being around Kate these past few days had been hard—far harder than he'd anticipated. He'd forgotten Kate's kind nature—or at least refused to remember it. How she had a way of connecting with people wherever she went. Like when she had chatted to the doorman at their hotel this evening, solicitously asking after his baby son. How did she even know he *had* one? And she had rushed to the aid of an elderly lady the other day, who hadn't been crossing the road quickly enough for impatient drivers. With her hands on her hips Kate had glared at the traffic, before helping the pensioner to the safety of the pavement, telling her to take all the time she needed. Miraculously, the tooting horns had stopped.

Nikos had been so sure he was over Kate O'Connor, so sure that she no longer meant anything to him, he'd thought he could have it tattooed across his forehead. But now doubts were creeping in. Doubts that he didn't want to acknowledge. Doubts that were driving him crazy. Despite keeping his distance, trying never to be alone with her, he was still falling under her spell.

After their hideous break-up, the shameful way Kate had treated him, he had returned to Greece, determined to put their short, disastrous relationship behind him. Pumped up with anger at Kate, for the whole degrading debacle, but most of all at himself for being such a damned fool, he had thrown himself into doing something he'd known he could make a success of—his business with Philippos.

To start with financial gain hadn't been the driving force behind their venture. It had been a welcome by-product, sure, but more important to Nikos had been utilising his business brain, taking Philippos's brilliant idea and turning it into a workable product. That was where the real satisfaction had lain for him.

But his ill-fated trip to New York had changed all that. Fiona O'Connor had immediately mercilessly exposed his naiveté about money, throwing his gullibility back in his face. She had made her pitifully low opinion of him abundantly clear and Kate had done absolutely nothing to back him up.

Because money *did* matter—Nikos knew that now. Money equalled power. And power meant that you had one hundred percent control over your own life. That no one could look down on you. No one could tell you that you weren't good enough. He might have come from a lowly background, and his own mother might not have wanted him, but money had meant he could rise above all that, invent a new persona. Money made you strong.

So Nikos had returned to Crete and set about making the fledgling business take off with a zeal that had bordered on the manic, pushing himself harder and harder, neglecting everything and everyone else in order to achieve his goal.

He had pushed Philippos too—something he now bitterly regretted. He had been part genius, part oddball, and Nikos should never have driven his friend so hard—never have bullied him into working faster, staying focussed. The sudden drive to make them both billionaires had been solely Nikos's obsession, and of no interest to the quiet and introspective Philippos.

But the business had taken off and the money had rolled in. And finally the power that Nikos had been seeking had been his. He had made it. And no one was ever going to make him feel unworthy again.

Least of all Kate O'Connor.

The problem was, she was making him feel a lot of other things… Nikos rubbed an impatient hand around the back of his neck. Faced with her again, he found he was battling all the same impulses, all the same desires. Bringing Kate back into his life had opened up all sorts of old wounds—wounds he'd convinced himself had long since healed. And he only had himself to blame. He'd been the one to set this whole thing up. If he'd done it as some sort of unconscious test then he was failing miserably. And that was something he needed to put right before they went any further.

One thing was for sure: he wouldn't be baring

his heart and soul again. He'd made that mistake once—never again. Ignoring his own set-in-concrete rules, he had offered Kate his love, his lifelong commitment. And what had she done in return? Ripped them to shreds and tossed them back in his face like worthless garbage. Kate had taught him a hard lesson—one he would never forget.

Now, as he covertly studied her from beneath half-closed eyes, Nikos could see the effort it was taking for her to politely clap along to the rowdy music, the forced half-smile on her face. She was hating this every bit as much as him. Well, *good*. It served her right.

Once he would have died for Kate O'Connor. Without a second's hesitation and without a heartbeat of doubt. Once she had meant everything to him. Now he had to guard against her power over him. He had to remember the reason they were here. Kate had been hired to serve a purpose, as a means to an end. That was all.

But the attraction was as strong as ever—Nikos couldn't deny that. Overwhelming, in fact. He could feel it like a pulse in his blood, raw and elemental, a carnal thrust that he couldn't contain. The thought of taking her to his bed was consuming him more and more, growing like a spreading stain.

But *if* it were to happen—and Nikos made himself emphasise the word *if*—then it would be strictly on his terms. That was a certainty.

Taking a sip of champagne, he set the glass down and pushed it away. Maybe instead of fighting the attraction he should be looking at it the other way. He now had Kate exactly where he wanted her. Whether it was by chance or through his own subliminal plotting, what did it matter?

No, not exactly where he wanted her. Nikos stole another glance. Where he wanted her wasn't here, in this crowded room full of ine-briated businessmen being entertained by ludi-crously dressed dancers. He wanted to be alone somewhere. Just him and her and enough time to make that really count.

The stirrings of desire made him shift his po-sition, adjust the fit of his trousers, before he let his eyes roam in her direction again. She sat very upright, her proud profile staring ahead, her hands clasped in her lap, until the last strains of the can-can finally died away and she raised them to clap politely again, her soft applause drowned out by the cheers of the crowd.

She couldn't wait for this to end—that much was obvious. As he watched she bent to pick up her purse and as she straightened up their eyes met. Those beautiful green eyes… For a moment he caught vulnerability there—a sort of lost helplessness that threatened to slash through his tough resolve. But a second later it was gone, replaced by the now familiar look of haughty disdain. A look that said she was tolerating him only because she had to, and even then, for the very least amount of time possible.

Well, they would see about that. This was starting to feel like a challenge—and Nikos had never been able to resist one of those.

Stepping out into the cool night air was a welcome relief after the claustrophobic atmosphere of the club. With the windmill still turning behind them, Nikos put their guests into a taxi, then took Kate's arm, tucking it against his side. He felt her stiffen but she didn't pull away.

He wasn't going to take her back to their hotel—not yet. He didn't want the evening to end with him knocking back another tumbler of whisky to try and numb his traitorous thoughts. The temptation of knowing that Kate was just the other side of that designer grey wall was enough to rob him of sleep if he didn't fight to control it. And enough to fill his dreams when he thought he had.

'Shall we take a walk?' He started to move them along the pavement, sidestepping the noisy crowd that were still spilling out of the club.

'If you like.'

It wasn't the most enthusiastic response to an invitation to accompany him on an evening stroll in the most romantic city in the world, but Nikos would take it. At least she wasn't arguing, and the crush on the pavement meant she had no alternative but to stay close by his side. He had no intention of letting her slip away now.

Kate breathed in the Parisian night air, concentrating on soaking up the atmosphere to try and blot out the nearness of the man beside her.

This place had such a buzz to it you couldn't help but fall in love with it. The ancient streets were bustling with tourists and locals alike, the cafés and restaurants were spilling out onto the wide pavements, the smell of cooking filled the air, laughter and chatter were all around them.

Turning a corner, they entered in a square filled with artists, their easels set up under trees festooned with fairy lights, their paintings spread out on the pavement or set up against the railings. Taking his cue from Kate, Nikos slowed his step.

'Montmartre is famous for its artists.' He gestured to the tall buildings around them. 'Renoir, Van Gogh, Picasso—they all lived and worked here at some point in their career.'

Kate followed his gaze. She was pretty good on her art history, so she already knew that, but how wonderful it was to think that these geniuses, whose paintings she had drooled over in galleries, had actually been here—maybe even stood in the exact same spot. She could almost feel their presence.

'Though I'm not sure these guys are quite in the same league.'

'Maybe not.' Kate gave a soft laugh. 'But they have to earn a living, the same as the rest of us, and if this is the way they do it then I envy them.'

'Really?' Nikos turned her towards him so he could see her face. 'You mean you would give up your candy empire in favour of an artist's palette?'

'It would be a camera in my case.' Kate pulled her gaze away from his searching stare. 'I would have loved to be a professional photographer.'

'But I thought you hated the paparazzi?'

'I do.' She turned back quickly to look at him. 'I'm not talking about that sort of photography. I mean portraits, landscapes—that sort of thing.'

'So why didn't you, then?'

'Why didn't I what?'

'Become a photographer?'

'As my father's only heir, I was expected to join the family firm. The idea was that I would start at the bottom, slowly learn all aspects of the business. But then Daddy died...' she looked away again '...and suddenly I was in charge of the whole company. Well, me and Mom. Mom couldn't cope with the pressure and I messed up—big-time. But I'm sure I don't need to tell *you* that.'

'No.' Nikos agreed, and his gentle voice turned her back to face him. 'There are plenty of sharks out there waiting for the chance to pounce on a vulnerable innocent.'

'As I found out to my cost.'

'Indeed.' Nikos scuffed his foot against the ground. 'But I always assumed taking control of Kandy Kate was what you wanted.'

'Maybe at some point in the future. But not

then. I never expected my father to die so soon…' Her voice tailed off.

'So your years of freedom were cut short?'

'I've never had any freedom—not really.' Kate met the dark gleam of his eyes. 'Kandy Kate has always ruled my life.'

As her gentle confession fell softly between them Nikos's intense stare made Kate catch her breath. For in that one fleeting moment it felt as if he was seeing the real her.

'And more so now than ever?' He lowered his head, deepening the level of intimacy.

'Yes…' The word came out on a soft breath. 'More so now than ever.'

'But it doesn't have to be like that.' Nikos shifted his position. 'Once I have legal guardianship of Sofia you will have your freedom back. Kandy Kate will be back on its feet. You could sell it as a profitable business, invest the money—do whatever you want to do.'

'I would never sell Kandy Kate.'

'No? Well, that's your choice.' His voice suddenly hardened, the glitter in his eyes turning to chips of ice. 'Why didn't you tell me, Kate, right from the start, that you were heiress to a confectionery fortune?'

'I told you about the business.' The mood had changed in an instant.

'But you deliberately played it down. I had no idea it was such a big deal until I got to New York.'

'I didn't think it was important.'

'Don't give me that,' Nikos scoffed. 'You consciously withheld the information.'

Kate touched her ear. 'Maybe I didn't tell you because I didn't want it come between us—the fact that...'

'Go on, Kate. The fact that what?'

'Well, that I was from a wealthy background and you were...'

'I was what? A penniless waiter? The son of a two-bit *taverna* owner?'

'No...well, yes. I didn't want the differences in our backgrounds to come between us.'

'*That* worked out well.' Sarcasm scored his voice. 'So I was right.' Nikos folded his arms across his chest. 'The reason you didn't want me to accompany you when you returned to New York was because you were ashamed of me.'

'No! You've got it all wrong, Nikos.'

'Really? Well, that's what it felt like. When I asked you to marry me, I had no idea of the extreme wealth of your family. When I flew to New York to attend your father's funeral I had no idea what I was walking in to. And that's because you deliberately kept it from me, Kate.'

'Well, if I did it was just because I was trying to hang on to what we had for as long as possible.'

'You *knew*, Kate. Right from the start you knew we had no long-term future. Even when you accepted my marriage proposal. Even as I slipped the engagement ring on your finger.'

'No! I didn't! You're twisting my words.'

'Then how come that ring had miraculously vanished by the time I arrived in New York?'

'You *know* why.' Kate looked down at her feet. 'When Daddy got ill, I didn't want to risk upsetting him any further...'

'Ah, yes. Thanks for that, Kate.'

'And then he died. And then...'

'Yeah.' Nikos curled his lip. 'I know—the rest is history.' He pushed back his shoulders, looking down at her from his imposing height. 'And now we're in the present and I'm the one with the money and the power. How does that feel, Kate?'

'It doesn't feel like anything.' Kate felt her

cheeks flush with the lie. 'You flatter yourself if you think you still have the ability to upset me.'

'Is that so?'

Cupping her jaw with one strong, warm hand, Nikos tilted her head until her startled gaze met his. She desperately battled against the pulse of arousal.

'Then you might want to tell your face.'

'I'm sorry?'

'That pinched expression is getting tiresome.'

What? Hurt and outrage stole away Kate's breath, along with the words she wanted to hurl at him.

But she had no chance to reply anyway. For Nikos had turned away, leaving Kate gaping at the broad width of his back as he strode towards a collection of paintings propped up against some railings. As he approached the artist—an elderly gentleman wearing a beret and a cotton jacket fastened with one high button—levered himself up from his stool and started a conversation.

Kate stayed where she was, silently seething. She saw the artist look over at her, say something to Nikos, then gesture for her to come closer. Reluctantly Kate did as she was told, keeping a frosty distance from Nikos, who was holding up a painting to inspect it more closely.

'Enchanté, mademoiselle.' With a theatrical flourish the artist took Kate's hand and raised it to his dry lips. Letting her hand drop, he took hold of her chin, turning her profile first one way and then the other. *'Magnifique.'* He muttered the word under his breath before addressing her again. 'The perfect artist's muse.'

'Thank you—*merci.*'

Kate flinched with embarrassment. No stranger to compliments, she usually casually accepted them for what they were—throwaway comments or chat-up lines. But this elderly gentleman seemed to be looking right through her.

'All the artists...they must be queuing up to paint you, *oui*?' He continued to stare at her.

'No—*non.*' She gave an awkward laugh. All she had was a controlling fake husband who thought she had a pinched face.

'Then I despair of the younger generation.' He shook his head sadly. 'If I were twenty years younger I would not let you walk away. But as it is...' He paused, stroking his chin. 'Perhaps you would allow me to do a drawing of you?'

'Oh, I don't think so...'

'Go on, Kate.' Nikos interrupted, a hint of amusement in his voice. 'Why not?'

'Ten minutes of your time—that's all.'

The artist was already clipping a large sheet of paper to his easel and picking up his charcoals. Gesturing to Kate to sit in a folding chair opposite him, he studied her carefully for several long seconds, then rapidly began to sketch.

Nikos moved so that he was behind the artist, his eyes travelling from the portrait to Kate and back again, almost as if he was drawing her himself. Kate held herself very still, Nikos's intense gaze was putting her in a sensual trance, making every inch of her feel tight, aware, as the sound of the charcoal squeaked across the paper. It was the most peculiar feeling.

'*Voilà.*' Unclipping the paper, the elderly man gave it a shake before turning it for Kate to see.

The trance broken, Kate looked at her image in astonishment. It was amazing, the way he had captured her so quickly and so accurately. Her guarded expression stared back at her, but there was also a faraway look in her eyes, a hint of the erotic way Nikos had made her feel as the sketch had been drawn. It was almost indecent—not to mention embarrassing. Kate had no idea she'd given away her feelings so blatantly. And if the artist had caught that look, then obviously so had Nikos.

She stole a nervous glance in his direction, but he was still standing in the shadows and she couldn't read his expression. Oh, well, Kate reasoned as she peered at the portrait again, on the plus side, at least Nikos couldn't accuse her of looking pinched.

'How much do I owe you?' Stepping forward, Nikos put his hand in his inside pocket, reaching for his wallet.

'*Rien*. Nothing.' The old man sprayed the portrait with fixative, then started to roll up it up, deftly tying it with string. 'This is a gift.'

'No, really—you must let me pay you.' Ever the alpha male, Nikos had pulled out a wad of euros and was trying to hand them over, but he was waved away dismissively.

'What you *must* do, *monsieur*, is take care of this young woman.' He solemnly presented Nikos with the drawing. 'Love her as she deserves to be loved. That is all the payment I need.'

Awkward!

After thanking the artist profusely, Kate moved away, suddenly desperate to escape the hothouse atmosphere surrounding them. She set off at a brisk pace, having no idea where she was going, but Nikos's footsteps soon caught up with her, and as he linked his arm through hers, guiding them away from the square, it was clear he was in charge again.

Kate's body stiffened as she waited for him to say something, to make a deliberate comment about the drawing that he held by its string in his left hand in order to watch her squirm. But seemingly lost in brooding silence Nikos remained quiet, and Kate let herself breathe again.

When she tried to loosen his hold on her, however, he resisted, keeping her securely by his side as he purposefully steered them through the narrow, twisty streets.

Eventually a steep fight of steps brought them to a wide open space, offering the most breathtaking view of Paris. Behind them the magnificent Basilica Sacré-Coeur rose up, floodlit a pale orange against the indigo night sky.

'Wow!' Kate whispered into the night as she stared in awe at the towering edifice.

'Quite something, isn't it?'

Despite his comment, Kate could feel that Nikos's intense gaze was focussed solely on her.

'Shall we walk up to the top?'

'Sure.' She hurriedly agreed, if only to stop him staring at her like that.

The shoes would have to go, though. All this walking in heels was killing her feet. Easing them off, she hooked them over her shoulder with two fingers, trying her best to ignore the fact that Nikos was watching her every move with meticulous attention.

The climb was well worth it. The view was even more spectacular from up here. The whole of Paris was laid out before them like a tapestry of light, with the Eiffel Tower twinkling away in the distance.

Kate sat herself down on the top step but Nikos seemed restless, pacing around with his arms folded across his chest. Eventually he came and sat next to her, so close that she could feel his warmth, breathe in his unique, intoxicating scent. Suddenly the view blurred and Kate became aware of nothing but the overpowering presence of the man beside her.

No matter where they were, however fraught, infuriating or downright horrific the situation, his nearness always provoked the same wild, uncontrollable reaction. A rioting mess of nerves and sensations that went through her like a sweeping storm, knotting her insides with both pleasure and pain, leaving her weak with longing.

She stole a look at his stark profile, softened only slightly by the glow from the floodlights. So darkly handsome. So imposing. Held in the quiet intensity of this moment, Kate heard herself silently wishing, yet again, that things could have been different. That they could have found a way to make it work.

As her gaze fell upon his proud features she was forced to accept that mistakes had been made on *both* sides. Nikos had been unforgivably cruel. But maybe she could have handled things better.

Dragging her gaze away to focus on the glittering lights of Paris, Kate knew one thing for certain. No matter what she did, how hard she tried to fight it, Nikos's grip on her heart refused to lessen.

CHAPTER SIX

NIKOS TOOK IN a sharp breath, hoping the chill of the night air would knock some sense into him. His agitation, far from lessening since they had left the Moulin Rouge, had only grown more intense. That old artist guy hadn't helped. He had fallen for Kate the same way everyone else seemed to. Something about her just drew people to her, made them love her.

Love her as she deserves to be loved.

Nikos turned the phrase over in his head. Hadn't he tried loving Kate once, with disastrous consequences? He had no intention of making that mistake again. What Kate *deserved* was to be treated the same way she had treated him. To be shown exactly what it felt like to be on the receiving end of such callous disregard.

He would never forgive her for the way she had treated him when he'd arrived in New York. The panicked look on her face when he'd introduced himself to her mother as her fiancé...the way she had rejected him, pushed him away, both as a lover and as a man, making it abundantly clear that he wasn't wanted there in the bosom of her precious family... It still trickled like lava through his veins. She had as good as told him he wasn't worthy of her love. Her crucifying lack of faith in him, in who he was and who he could be, had ripped their precious relationship to shreds, tearing it apart like tissue paper.

Yes, Kate O'Connor deserved to be taught a lesson. And the form that lesson should take loomed larger and larger in Nikos's head. The longer he was in Kate's presence, the harder it became to resist.

He needed a diversion. Taking a breath, Nikos marshalled his thoughts into line. He needed something to diffuse the insidious power Kate had over him. *Fiona O'Connor*. The thought of that woman should do it.

'So...' Nikos gave a small cough. 'How is your mother?' His random question sounded every bit as insincere as it was. But immediately Kate's head flew in his direction.

'She's okay, thank you.'

'I trust she won't get her hands on any of the money I have invested in Kandy Kate?'

Kate gave a huff. 'So *that's* what you're worrying about? Let me assure you, your investment is perfectly safe.'

'*Kalos*—good.' Nikos placed his hand on the step between them. It felt pleasantly cold beneath his touch. 'Though you can't blame me for checking. I have to say the way she managed to ruin the reputation of the family business so quickly was very impressive. Her quote about never letting you eat candy as a kid because it was so bad for your teeth was a masterstroke.'

'She was tricked into saying that by a manipulative journalist.'

'Still defending her, Kate?' Nikos edged closer, enjoying himself now. He watched as Kate picked up her shoes from beside her and placed them in her lap. 'You still think that Mommy Dearest has done nothing wrong?'

'I know she made some bad decisions. We both did.'

'You can say that again.'

A tense silence split the air before Kate stood up, the shoes still held in her hands. She raised one, almost like a weapon, before bending to slip it onto her foot, wobbling unsteadily. Immediately Nikos was there, his arms around her to steady her.

'But now you're able to put that right.' He held her firmly to him, refusing to let her pull away. She felt slight beneath his touch—fragile like a trapped bird. 'I know how much that means to you.'

'Yes.' Kate held herself very still, her green eyes flashing in the dark. 'It means everything.'

'Everything?' Nikos turned the word over in his mouth. It left a bitter taste. 'That just about sums it up, doesn't it, Kate? If only you'd told me that from the start it would have saved a lot of…' He hesitated momentarily as he banished the word *heartache* from his lips. 'A lot of confusion.'

He felt Kate stir in his arms, inhaled the meadowy scent of her freshly washed hair.

'Let me go, Nikos.'

Nikos released his grip, letting his hands slide down Kate's bare arms and at the last minute taking hold of her hands in his. 'I thought I'd done that a long time ago, Kate. I really did.' He stared at their joined hands, his thumbs gently stroking her palms. 'Now I'm not so sure.'

Slowly, deliberately, he raised his eyes to meet hers.

'What do you mean by that?'

Kate's voice was wary, but the wild flash in her eyes shot a message straight to Nikos's groin.

'I mean that now we've become reacquainted I find there are ghosts that need to be put to rest.' He held himself still.

'There's no such thing as ghosts.'

Pulling her hands free, Kate folded them across her chest, pushing up the soft swell of her breasts. The amber light played across the angles of her bare shoulders, her breastbone, shadowing the hollows, emphasising the pale, silky skin.

'I'm sure your mother told you that.'

'My mother never told me anything.' The need to control that kick of lust made his voice harsher, more impassioned than he'd intended. 'She upped and left long before we had the chance to have cosy bedtime chats about such things.'

'I thought you said she died when you were a teenager?' Immediately Kate pounced on his confession.

'She did.' Nikos held his voice firm. 'But she left me and my father long before that. On my second birthday, in fact. Impeccable timing. From that day on I never saw her again.'

'Oh, I'm sorry, Nikos. I didn't know.' Kate's

green eyes filled with concern. 'Why have you never told me that before?'

Nikos let out a sharp breath. 'I hardly think you're in a position to criticise me for withholding information about my family.' His mocking jibe hit its target full-on. 'And, just in case you were in any doubt, I don't want your sympathy either. If anything, I should be feeling sorry for *you*.'

'Me? Why?'

'For having a mother like Fiona. If she's an example of maternal virtues, I'm better off without.'

He saw Kate flinch, almost as if he had hit her. Maybe his comment had been below the belt, but Nikos told himself that didn't mean Kate didn't deserve it. She had sided with her mother right from the start, and made no attempt to ease the shock of that first meeting—a hugely awkward situation entirely of Kate's making. Not only that, but she had bundled him away out of sight like a dirty secret, like something shameful. She had given him no chance to try and win Fiona round.

Nikos didn't give a damn what Fiona O'Connor thought of him. He hadn't back then and he didn't now. Sure, he'd been shocked by her reaction to him. But he would have brushed that aside, ignored her vituperative comments, laughed them off—*if* he'd had Kate's support. He'd naively thought the love they shared was rock-solid, for ever, strong enough to withstand the strongest onslaught. Let alone a self-obsessed middle-aged woman with a dislike of young, penniless Greeks.

How wrong he'd been. Kate's love had disappeared at the first sign of trouble. Or maybe it had never been there at all.

As he stared at her now he felt memories flooding back unbidden, the old anger slamming into him hot and hard, tightening his skin. What was he talking about? Of *course* it had never been there. Hadn't Kate made that perfectly obvious when he had walked into her room on the night of her father's funeral?

That torturous day.

Seeing Kate in such agonising pain had been terrible for Nikos to watch. She had seemed so alone—as if she'd had to shoulder the weight of Bernie's death for both her *and* her mother. Nikos had seen that she was completely consumed by her sorrow, hollowed out by it, a mere shell of the warm, vibrant, funny young woman he had met in Crete. He had longed to comfort her, to support her, to be there for her as her fiancé.

But Kate had pushed him away, rejected everything he had tried to do for her, all his attempts to comfort her—almost as if she'd blamed him for her father's death. Or just blamed him for being *there*. For turning up in New York when she had told him to stay at home. For threatening the precariously balanced equilibrium of the O'Connor family. For being the lowly, worthless no-hoper they clearly thought he was.

Completely sidelined, Nikos had swallowed his pride and retreated into the shadows, not wanting to cause Kate any more grief than she'd been suffering already. Their engagement had been conveniently pushed aside, with Kate telling her mother with flustered insistence that she wasn't to worry about it, only just stopping short of saying Nikos had made it all up. And Nikos had been effectively banished. Ignored.

He had slept in the spare room, sat at the back at the funeral service, kept out of everyone's way at the wake, watching from a distance as Kate behaved socially, comforting her wailing mother, playing host to all the mourners. But by the time the last guest had gone the strain of the day had been written all over her face, pulling her facial muscles taut, hollowing her cheeks. And Nikos had hated to see her like that.

So that night, after Kate had excused herself and gone to her room, he had decided to go after her, intending to do nothing more than put his arms around her, hold her tight, try and take away a little of her pain.

There had been no reply when he'd tapped on the door, so he had quietly let himself in. The room had been empty, but as Nikos had stood there in the doorway Kate had appeared from the bathroom, with something in her hand. She had jumped when she saw him.

'Nikos!'

'Hi.' He'd advanced into the room, itching to put his arms around her. 'I didn't mean to startle you. I just wanted to check you're okay.'

'Yes, I'm fine.' Her hands had gone behind her back.

'No, you're not Kate.' He had stood in front of her, looking down at her slender figure dressed in cream satin pyjamas. 'You are far from fine.'

'I just need to get some sleep, that's all.'

'Right.' Nikos had put his hands on her shoulders, and as she'd tensed beneath his touch she had inflicted another wound on his pride. 'So I'm being dismissed, is that it?'

Kate had given a heavy sigh. 'I don't want to argue, Nikos.'

He'd felt her shoulders shrug.

'Neither do I. I'm trying to *help*, Kate, to do whatever I can to support you.'

'Like I said, I just need some rest.' She'd released one hand from behind her back and tucked her hair behind her ear. 'It's been a long day...' Her voice had tailed off.

'Very well.' Nikos had swallowed down the hurt of her words. 'I'll go. Right after you've told me what you're hiding behind your back.'

Kate had flushed. The first colour he'd seen in her cheeks since he'd arrived.

'Nothing.'

Holding out his hand, palm upright, Nikos had done his best to suppress his irritation. He'd already had a good idea what it was, and he'd had no intention of being frozen out. He'd felt his heart begin to thud.

Realising there was no way out, Kate had slowly brought her arm round to her front. Nikos had seen the pale column of her throat as she'd swallowed, but it had been the look in her eyes that had sent ice through his veins. *Fear.* No—more than that. *Panic.* She'd been almost shaking with it.

He'd looked down at the little plastic stick in her hand. A swirl of emotions had run through him, too fast and too unexpected to be able to process in the time allowed.

Instead he had cleared his throat. 'Let me see.'

He had fully expected Kate to argue, but instead she had submissively handed it over, as if all the fight had left her.

A diagram beside the little window on the stick had helpfully explained the result. Two pink lines; pregnant. One pink line; not pregnant.

Nikos had raised his eyes to find Kate staring not at the test stick but straight at him, a wild look in her eyes.

'Well?' Her anguished cry had made it clear she didn't know the result.

'You are not pregnant, Kate.'

'Oh, thank God.' With a gasp of relief Kate had taken the test from him, stared at it, then sunk to her knees.

Nikos had stared down at the top of her head,

at the way the overhead light shone on the glossy chestnut hair that fell over her shoulders. And something had stirred inside him. The unfamiliar sensation had quickly gathered power as the events of the past few days had flashed before him, firing his temper, draining his self-control.

Suddenly he'd seen the way he had behaved for what it was—*weakness*. Not the compassion he had convinced himself he had to find as he had bitten his tongue, turned the other cheek. He had been treated like dirt by Fiona. Coldly distanced by Kate as if he was nothing…no one… their engagement brushed under the carpet. All this he had accepted because Kate had lost her beloved father. Telling himself she was grieving. That he had to give her time.

But this. This was the final straw.

'I take it you're pleased?' His voice had been dangerously thin as he'd tried to gather together the threads of his composure.

'Of course.' Kate had looked up at him in surprise. 'To get pregnant now would have been a disaster.'

'A disaster?'

The word had felt like a stone in his mouth. With a sickening wave of realisation, Nikos had known he would never have seen it like that. Far from it. After the initial shock he would have been pleased, proud. Ecstatic, even. The thought of creating a new life with Kate, of being a father, would to him have been an exciting adventure he couldn't wait to embark on. A few weeks ago he'd have been sure that Kate would react the same way. And yet here she was, treating the idea of being pregnant with his baby as if it would be some sort of ghastly ordeal.

With a bitter twist of resentment Nikos had seen that once again he was being betrayed by a woman he loved. His mother had rejected him as a son—now Kate was rejecting him as a father.

He should have dropped the subject, walked away, left the discussion for another more appropriate time. But somehow he hadn't been able to. His pride hadn't let him.

'Can I ask why you would have considered it a disaster?' There had been an edge of warning in his tone.

'Well, that's obvious, isn't it?' Kate had clearly chosen to ignore his warning, which had only inflamed his temper still further.

'Not to me, it's not.'

'I could never have coped with a baby on top

of everything else.' She'd sighed heavily. 'Now that Daddy is…no longer here, I'm going to have to take over the running of the business, concentrate on looking after my mother. She needs me now more than ever.'

'And our family? Or what might have been our family…?' He'd gestured to the test stick that had lain discarded on the sumptuous cream carpet. 'That would count for nothing?'

Kate had wearily shaken her head. 'Look, I can't do this now, Nikos. Just be grateful that I'm not pregnant and let's leave it at that.'

She'd extended her arm, her palm facing him, the gesture intended to tell him to go away. To shoo him out like a worthless piece of garbage. As if he was nothing.

And something inside Nikos had snapped. Because if he hadn't already been infuriated enough, in Greece that gesture meant something else entirely. It was about as insulting as you could get. And even though he'd known Kate wasn't aware of that, Nikos had still found himself seething with anger, the pride in him rising to the surface.

'Trust me—I *am* grateful!'

He'd taken hold of her hand, dropping it down

by her side. Kate's eyes had flashed with surprise and something else—shock. *Good.* It was high time she took notice of him. Showed him some respect. Nikos had had precious little of that since he'd arrived at the O'Connor residence.

'No doubt you are relieved that I won't be tainting your precious O'Connor blood with my lowly genes, but let me tell you this.' He'd pointed a finger to where Kate stood rooted to the spot in shocked silence. 'I am *glad* you are not pregnant, because I wouldn't want any child of mine burdened with *you* as a mother.'

'Nikos!'

'I mean it, Kate.' The fire raged had through him, ringing in his ears, scraping his skin. 'You may think you're better than me. That all *this…*' he'd gestured to the opulent room, the enormous windows offering a panoramic view of Central Park and the New York skyline '…makes you superior in every way. Well, let me tell you something. You are mistaken. I may not come from a moneyed family, and I haven't had a privileged upbringing like you, but you know what? I'm glad. Because I have something way more important—principles, honour and integrity.'

'And you think I don't?' Her voice had been very small.

'I think you've lost sight of what matters, Kate. You can't see what's right in front of you.'

'Which is…?'

'That you are nothing more than the spoilt little girl of a doting daddy and a manipulative mummy.' His mouth had hardened. 'I didn't know your father, but…'

Kate had made a low noise, like the soft grunt of a wounded animal. Her hand had felt for the dresser beside her. 'D-don't you d-dare disrespect my father.' She'd gulped out the words.

Nikos had paused, Kate's paper-thin fragility momentarily halting the rollercoaster of his rage at the top of the track. He'd lowered his voice. 'All I'm saying is, if he was the great guy you say he was he didn't deserve a wife and daughter like you.'

Silence had fallen between them as sharp as jagged glass. Kate had taken a staggering step away from him.

'I see now that the woman I met in Crete—the woman I fell in love with—never really existed.' Nikos had ruthlessly continued. 'She was a fake, a phony. Beneath that free spirit hid the real Kate

O'Connor. Someone who was just having bit of fun before settling down to marry a rich banker from a nice solid American family. Am I right?'

Kate's eyes had darted frantically across his face. 'If you truly believe that, Nikos, then you don't know me at all.'

'No?' He would show her no mercy. 'Or does being faced with the truth hurt, Kate?'

'Everything hurts.'

Her simple statement, the tortured look on her face, had torn into Nikos so that he'd almost weakened. *Almost.*

But suddenly Kate had rallied, moving over to the door and flinging it open with the last of her strength.

'Get out.'

'Very well.'

He had been beside her in a couple of strides. When she'd refused to look at him he'd reached out, gently raising her chin with a single finger-tip, searching her eyes. His heart had slowed to a dull beat at the huge significance of that moment.

'But just so you know, Kate, if I leave now I won't be coming back.'

He'd waited, his breath locked in his chest.

Waited for Kate to say something, to do something to stop this landslide of misery.

But instead she had remained silent. A silence that had pressed down on him more firmly with every passing second.

'If I walk out now our relationship will be over.'

He'd driven home the point to make sure she understood, forcing the words through a closing throat, through lips tight with concealed emotion.

And as Kate had looked up at him he'd seen the truth, heard the words before they were spoken.

Her lower lip had wobbled, her voice had cracked, but her eyes had been like stone. 'Our relationship is over already, Nikos.'

Three years might have passed since then, but as Nikos stared at Kate now he knew that the brutal emotions of that night were not dead and buried. Far from it. One heavy look from those sea-green eyes, one whisper of her breath against his cheek, one pout of those soft, sexy lips and he was right back there. Caught up in her power. He might be older now, and he was certainly richer, but where Kate was concerned he was no wiser.

He took in a breath of the sweet night air, silently cursing the way Kate held his gaze, looking at him with a wide-eyed honesty that was guaranteed to mess with his head even more. She wasn't being deliberately provocative. If anything she appeared nervous, unsure, standing there with the whole of Paris behind her, her head slightly to one side, her mouth tightly closed.

She held herself carefully, as if she didn't trust her high heels on these uneven ancient steps. Or she didn't trust herself. Which made Nikos's libido soar even further off the scale.

He had to find some control—fast.

Pushing back his shoulders, he marshalled his behaviour into line. 'It's getting late. We should be heading back to the hotel.'

He turned abruptly and started down the steps, without looking at Kate, without waiting for her to reply. Because if she subjected him to so much as a hint of temptation as to what might happen back at the hotel, where this night might end, he was a dead man.

CHAPTER SEVEN

RAISING HER CAMERA, Kate took another great shot. It was almost too easy—Venice had to be the most beautiful place in the world. Paris had not disappointed her, nor Rome, from what she had managed to see during the whirlwind couple of days she and Nikos had spent there. But Venice took her breath away.

Behind her the gondolier, wearing the traditional blue-and-white-striped jumper, skilfully manoeuvred their gondola through the busy traffic of the Grand Canal, pointing out various landmarks. The grand *palazzos* and the Baroque churches, the Doge's Palace, the Rialto Bridge... There was something stunning everywhere she looked—like the most glamorous film set brought to life.

Taking a sharp turn off the main thoroughfare, the gondolier started down a smaller canal, so narrow in places that he had to use his hands to push away from the sides of the ancient buildings to keep their course straight. Away from the hustle and bustle, all was peaceful—just the soothing sound of the oar in the water, muffled voices in the distance. These were the back streets of Venice and, to Kate, every bit as fascinating as the showy Grand Canal.

Craning her neck, she gazed up at the old buildings with their wrought-iron balconies and wooden shutters flaking with peeling paint. She wondered what it would be like to live there, whether the people behind those walls were happy. Everybody had their problems—she knew that. Sometimes she just felt as if she had more than her fair share.

As they approached a low bridge Kate turned to look at the gondolier. Standing on the stern, he was going to have to be careful not to bang his head. They were gliding ever closer, and he seemed to be paying no heed, but at the last second he gave her a wink and ducked his head. Smiling, Kate turned back to the front—and immediately found herself caught in the glare of Nikos's penetrating gaze, with the shadow of the bridge crossing his face as they glided underneath.

His expression was hard to read—neither cold

nor friendly, but more like deliberately watchful, as if he wanted her to know that he noticed everything…even a cheeky wink from a Venetian gondolier.

Since that night on the steps of the Sacré-Coeur, there had been no more in-depth conversations, no more mention of her family, for which Kate was very grateful. Nikos's brutal assessment of her mother had wound her tighter than a sprung coil, just as he had intended it to, but deep down she could see that his views were justified. Fiona had treated him appallingly.

So had she, come to that.

Maybe if she had been able to explain her mother's situation to Nikos things would have been different. But Fiona had made her swear that under no circumstances was Kate *ever* to tell *anyone* about her condition. Trying to reason with her, impress upon her the fact that mental illness was nothing to be ashamed of, had had the reverse effect, with her mother becoming increasingly hysterical because Kate wanted to tell everyone that she was 'crazy'. That she wouldn't be happy until her mother had been locked away.

So Kate had obeyed her and kept quiet. It was

her mother's illness after all, not hers. She'd had to respect her wishes.

Kate's relationship with Fiona had always been a difficult one. As a child she had accepted that her mother was 'delicate'—that she would sometimes spend days in bed, suffering with headaches, baffling mood swings. Her father had impressed upon Kate that her mom had to be treated with the utmost care, obeyed at all times and kept calm. It hadn't been until she was a teenager that Kate had realised there was a medical reason for all that. Fiona suffered from anxiety and depression.

As the face of Kandy Kate, Kate had spent her young life on a constant round of photo shoots and advertising campaigns, all orchestrated by her mother. This role, it seemed, was the one thing that had given Fiona a focus, helped keep her demons at bay. So Kate had done as she was told.

When other kids had been out on their bikes, she'd been having her nails manicured. When they'd been having fun at sleepovers, she'd been tucked up in bed. Because her mother had insisted on her looking perfect at all times. It had almost felt as if Fiona's life depended on it.

The pattern of subservience to her mother had continued all through Kate's teenage years and into her early twenties. With her father's unconditional love she had had at least one parent she could turn to for a cuddle, for comfort and advice. But Bernie had also had Fiona's moods to consider, and because Kate had wanted to try and make life easier for him she had striven to be the perfect daughter. Never once had she rocked the boat.

She'd been twenty-three when her father had suggested she come into the business with him. Having studied photography at university, she'd fancied a career travelling the world, doing photo shoots in faraway exotic locations. But duty had called. Her father had needed her.

So they had struck a deal. Kate would go travelling for three months, and then join the firm when she returned.

Fiona, however, had not been happy with this arrangement. She'd seen no reason for Kate to go 'gallivanting off' to Europe. She'd thought there was nothing to be gained by letting her go, and that Bernie was simply 'indulging' his daughter.

Maybe she'd feared that Kate would never come back—who knew? But for once Bernie had put his foot down, insisting that Kate was to be allowed this one taste of freedom. He and Fiona had fought—a terrible row that had seen Fiona sobbing and screaming all night, punctuated only by Bernie's angry voice. A booming tone that Kate had never heard before.

Desperate to make peace, Kate had offered to abort her travel plans immediately. But her father had had none of it. He had insisted she was still going. That her mother would get over it. That everything would be all right.

But of course it hadn't been all right. Six weeks later, when Kate had been having so much fun, free from the shackles of Kandy Kate, revelling in her freedom, *falling in love*, her father had had a heart attack. From which he had never recovered.

Returning to New York, Kate had found her mother in a dangerously unstable state, hurling accusations at her, saying that *she* was responsible for her father's heart attack. That it would never have happened if Kate hadn't been such a selfish, irresponsible child, going off to Europe and causing so much trouble.

Racked with worry and crippling grief since Bernie had died, Kate had soon had guilt to contend with too. She'd known her priority had to be her mother. That she'd have to do everything she could to try and help Fiona through this—stop her from sliding into utter despair. Her own heartache would have to be put aside. At least for the time being.

Nikos, too, had had to be locked away in her heart. And Kate had vowed keep him there until the dust had settled. Until she could find the right time. Until Fiona was strong enough to hear the news that she had fallen in love with a carefree Greek Adonis. That she was engaged to be married.

Kate had known for certain that her mother would need a lot of careful handling on that one…

But then Nikos had turned up and put the cat amongst the pigeons. With Fiona's reaction to their engagement predictably volatile, Kate had stepped between them, taking the verbal blows as Fiona had demanded to know what Kate thought she was doing, bringing this good-for-nothing creature into their family, being so stupid as to imagine she could *marry* such a man. Didn't Kate realise he was only after her money? Hadn't Kate done enough damage already?

She had already killed her father. Did she want to have her mother's death on her conscience too?

She didn't really mean it, Kate had told herself. It was the shock talking… Intense grief coupled with Fiona's fragile mental health made her say those hurtful things.

But it had still been a desperate situation, and Kate had known she had to focus all her attention on her mother. She simply hadn't had the energy to worry about Nikos right then. Hadn't he made everything worse by turning up uninvited, anyway?

So Kate had pushed him away, minimised his significance in her life as she'd battled to cope with the trauma all around her. She'd seen the hurt in those deep brown eyes but had refused to process it. She hadn't been able to cope with any more stress. Nikos was strong…their love was strong, or so she'd thought. Later she would explain, make it up to him. Her mother was her top priority.

And on top of all that there had been something else niggling away at Kate. When exactly had she had her last period? She hadn't been able to remember for sure, but knew it must have been before her father was taken ill. The thought of telling Fiona she was pregnant with Nikos's baby was too stressful to contemplate. Her mother would go berserk.

Kate had genuinely started to worry that Fiona's prediction might come true. She might be responsible for her mother's death, too.

So Kate had squashed down any excitement, banished any silly dreams about the beautiful baby she and Nikos might have, and convinced herself the test had to be negative. Which was why she'd been so relieved when it was. She had genuinely thought Nikos would be too. How wrong she had been!

His bitter, vicious reaction had taken her completely by surprise. To this day she still didn't know what had triggered it. But she had no intention of asking him now. You didn't poke a hornets' nest unless you wanted to get stung.

Even though they had both refrained from dragging up the past again since Paris, Nikos was far from letting Kate off the hook. The whole time they had been together on this phony honeymoon—wherever they went, whatever they did—he monitored her every move, his eyes all over her, all the time. Part alarming, part seductive, Kate didn't know which was the scarier emotion. But she did know that the power of those deep brown eyes set her body on fire, quickening her pulse, tightening her core, and that whenever she looked up to find him staring at her she felt the sweep of his gaze skitter over her skin.

Like right now.

The vibe between them here in Venice was different, somehow. Last night they had actually dined together, just the two of them, in a gorgeous little *trattoria* tucked away down a side canal, far from the hustle and bustle of the glitzy tourist spots. To Kate's surprise there had been no photographers either, but she had resisted the temptation to ask Nikos why this was and given herself permission to relax and actually enjoy the evening.

They'd kept away from the danger topics and conversation had flowed freely, Nikos making Kate laugh with his irreverent sense of humour, reminding her of the man she had first met and fallen for so hard and so fast. But at the end of the night the shutters had clattered down again. The heady cocktail of desire and longing that had been swirling around them all evening had been pushed firmly back into its box.

Kate was left with the scary realisation that she had absolutely no idea what went on in the darkly handsome head of Nikos Nikoladis. But she did know that as the days passed, the more time she spent in his company, the more temptingly dangerous it felt.

All too soon their gondola trip was over, and as they arrived back at the dock the gondolier leapt onto the wooden steps and held out a hand to Kate. Thanking him with her few words of Italian, Kate smiled as he kissed her hand, bowing with a theatrical flourish before helping her ashore.

With his back towards her, Nikos was giving the man a tip—a surprising amount, judging by the look on the gondolier's face. Nikos said something—Kate couldn't make out what—and the two men shook hands.

'So...' Nikos took Kate's arm to guide her up the steps. 'Am I to be constantly warning off your amorous suitors when we are out together?'

'What do you mean?' She looked at him in surprise.

'Well, it seems that wherever we go you have men flirting outrageously with you.'

'Don't exaggerate.' Kate gave a small laugh, adjusting the neck of her blouse. 'It's just the Italian way.'

'Hmm…' Nikos mused quietly. 'And what if I don't like it?'

They were walking arm in arm towards St Mark's Square, and it was funny how natural that felt, but Nikos's remark halted Kate's step.

'Why would you care?' She turned her green eyes to meet his, her question gentler than she'd expected. The feminist in her was obviously taking a day off.

'I'm not sure.' Nikos held her gaze. 'I've been asking myself the same question.'

'And have you come up with an answer?'

'Not really, no.' Nikos started walking again. 'Sometimes it's best not to overanalyse these things.

That was probably good advice. Kate had no desire to analyse why his unexpected possessiveness curled so warmly inside her.

They entered the famous square, pigeons scattering at their feet.

'What did you say to that gondolier, anyway?' She brought herself back into line.

'I told him to back off if he knew what was good for him.'

'You didn't!' Kate stared at him in outrage.

'Or maybe I just thanked him for an excellent trip. Which do *you* think it was, Kate?'

'I… I don't know.'

But one look at the supercilious smirk on Nikos's face and she did know. He was winding her up. God, he was infuriating.

'Shall we get a cup of coffee?' He gestured to the crowded café tables at the sides of the square.

Kate shook her head. 'I want to take a few more photos, but you go ahead.'

What she really wanted was some space to draw a badly needed breath, to try and numb the alarming effect he was having on her. This provocative, teasing Nikos was messing with her head even more than the coldly calculating one she had been faced with at the start of their grand tour. And not just her head…

Kate could feel his dangerous presence insidiously invading every part of her body, further wearing down her defences with every hour that passed. Weakening them with every wicked glint from those midnight eyes, every purposeful twitch of that seductive mouth, every gesture of those expressive hands.

There was no doubt that he was still the most drop-dead gorgeous man she had ever met in her life. His beauty held her spellbound, the sheer perfection of him captivating her as surely as a net thrown over a helpless animal. But what Kate felt for Nikos went way deeper than physical attraction. Somehow he had touched a part of her she hadn't even known existed. Awakened something she hadn't known was there. And now it refused to die.

If Kate had ever thought she could escape from the hold he had over her she now knew she'd been wrong. And, scarier still, she wasn't even sure she wanted to.

Making herself concentrate on taking pictures, Kate strolled around the square, shading her eyes to gaze up at the soaring bell tower, admiring the way the sunlight glinted off the gilded flanks of the four enormous horses above the entrance to the Basilica. There was no shortage of things to photograph—everywhere she looked there was a potentially stunning shot.

She didn't know exactly where Nikos was sitting having his coffee, and there was no way she was going to seek him out, but she still felt as if his eyes were following her around—as if he was the marksman and she was his target. She was still obsessively aware of him even when he wasn't there.

Photographs done, she replaced the lens cap and pushed back her shoulders. The sunshine was warm, and she was starting to regret her decision to wear leather trousers. Shorts would have been a better choice...or something cotton and floaty.

'Did you get the shots you wanted?'

Her temperature only soared higher as Nikos came to stand beside her, sliding a strong arm around her waist. Kate looked around, expecting to see a photographer lurking somewhere, assuming this must be another photo op orchestrated by Nikos in his relentless pursuit of generating favourable publicity for his cause. But there was no photographer—just a sea of tourists, much like themselves, going about their business.

Silently Nikos's hand dipped lower, settling on her hip, his fingers spreading so that they curved over the top of her bottom. Each and every one of Kate's muscles went into spasm.

'Yes, thanks.' She held herself very still, fighting the burn of his touch. It felt like a deliberate test, to see how she would react.

When he took his hand away she allowed herself a quick breath, but now his fingers were inching under the hem of her blouse, finding their way to the bare skin of her waist, whispering over her flesh. And then Kate did react—she felt a rush of blood spreading to her core.

She could have so easily pulled away. But with his caress like velvet against her overheated skin she found herself edging closer to him, inviting his hand to move further under her blouse, to find more of her over-sensitised flesh.

'You feel a little warm, *agape mou*.' Nikos slanted her a lazy smile, and there was more than a hint of triumph in his eyes. 'Shall we go somewhere to cool down?'

Swallowing hard, Kate took a step away. 'I might go back to the hotel to change. I hadn't realised the weather would be so hot.'

'It's true.' His dark eyes were heavy with seduction. 'The temperature *does* seem to have shot up.'

They started back in the direction of their hotel, walking quickly, dodging tourists, as if a sudden unspoken purposefulness was moving them forward.

The hotel lobby was cool and dark after the brightness outside. Set directly on the Grand Canal, The Palazzo, with its Baroque architecture and opulent furnishings, had to be one of the most exclusive hotels in Venice. But for some reason it only had a teeny-tiny elevator. As the door slid closed behind them and Nikos towered over her, radiating heat and hunger and pure sexual magnetism, Kate felt the small amount of oxygen in it vanish completely.

Nikos fixed Kate with a direct stare, watching with male satisfaction at the way her breasts hitched beneath the heat of his gaze, listening with quiet pleasure to the small gasp of her shortened breath. Neither of them said anything, but as the elevator groaned its way to the penthouse suite there was no mistaking the heavy thud of desire beating between them.

He adjusted his weight, impatient now, his need rapidly overtaking his anticipation, delicious though it was. Never far from the surface, his hunger for Kate had ramped up painfully that morning when she'd appeared wearing those black trousers. That leather-clad butt had been tormenting him all day, and turning other men's heads in her direction too—even more so than usual.

Nikos didn't like that. He had only been half joking when he'd made that quip about warning off amorous suitors. Watching her walking around St Mark's Square being ogled by every red-blooded chancer in the place had set his blood simmering, until eventually he'd had no choice but to stride over to claim her for himself, his hand on her backside branding her as his. And the reality hadn't disappointed. Feeling her muscles tighten beneath his touch had spread a fire to his groin that still burned, hot and fierce.

But it had left him wanting more—much more. And he wanted it *now*.

Their suite was dark and quiet when they entered, the maid having closed the shutters against the sun. Neither of them made any move to open them.

Nikos stood in front of Kate, still not touching her, just waiting. His eyes travelled to the front of her pretty chiffon blouse. The top three buttons were undone, he noticed, revealing the very edge of a pink lacy bra. He swallowed.

Their eyes met again, but still neither of them moved.

'Nikos...'

Never had his name on a woman's lips sounded quite so sinfully seductive. The blood in his veins slowed to a sluggish crawl, as if preparing itself for a very particular exertion, while the crotch of his jeans tightened painfully.

He waited, the air in the room pressing down on him. And when she said nothing he prompted her. 'Kate?'

'Nikos, I... I...'

'Yes?' The agony and the ecstasy of the wait was all but killing him. But wait he would. For Kate to come to him.

He closed his eyes for a moment, as if to make it easier for her. There was a faint rustle, the sense of a vacuum being filled, and then the sweet, soft whisper of her breath on his neck. Nikos opened his eyes. Kate was right in front of him, gazing up at him, her pupils so dilated that her dark green eyes were almost black. Her mouth was slightly open—a soft, sensual pout, waiting to be claimed.

When she raised herself on to her tiptoes, bringing her upturned face within inches of his, Nikos finally let go—finally gave himself permission to do what he had been wanting to do so badly for the last hour, the last week...ever since he had set eyes on Kate again in that revolting club.

His mouth came down on hers in a bruising kiss, his hands spanning her waist to pull her closer to him, then moving down to feel that leather-clad bottom again. *And, God, did it feel good.*

Pressing her against him, he let his lips glory in the feel of her soft mouth, the way it opened for him, passionately kissing him back. A thousand memories crashed through him—the taste of her, the feel of her, the way she fitted her body so perfectly to his. Everything she did to him. The way she always had. Right from that very first time.

The urge to make love to Kate when they had first met had been overpowering, all-consuming. Even though he'd guessed she was far less sexually experienced than him she had left it until the very last minute—literally the point of no return—to tell him she was actually a virgin.

Grappling with a desire so strong it had blurred his vision, Nikos had tried to hold back, tried to make sure it was what she really wanted. That even though they had only just met she was certain she wanted to give herself to him. And Kate had laughed softly, cupping his cheeks in her hands, smothering his face with wet kisses, urging him to take her there and then. No doubts, no second thoughts.

And take her he had.

Nothing had prepared him for the power of their union. It had completely blown him away. Sex with Kate had been so much more than three little letters. So much more than it had ever been with anyone else. Totally absorbed by her and the strength of their passion, it had felt like the smallest step for Nikos to decide he had to make her his for ever. To ask her to be his wife.

Three years later and Kate was finally bound to him. But the circumstances couldn't be more different. Gone was the starry-eyed joy, the bluebirds tweeting overhead, the silhouetted image of them set against a rosy sunset. What a fool he had been to have thought that was possible—with Kate or anyone else. Hadn't his parents' disastrous relationship taught him *anything*?

According to his father, theirs had been a crazy, mad love affair, full of fire and passion. And look how *that* had ended. Spectacularly imploding when his mother hadn't been able to take the responsibility of raising a child—raising him.

And Nikos had stupidly done exactly the same thing—fallen for the wrong woman, rushed blindly into a doomed relationship, all the lessons of his past forgotten. Only he and Kate hadn't even made it as far as having a child. The look on Kate's face of immense relief on discovering she wasn't pregnant with his baby still had the power to knife him in the guts.

But this wasn't about confronting those demons. He had no intention of wasting a second of this precious window of time in trying to unknot their twisted past. He was going to live this moment as if it were his last.

As he felt for the buttons of her blouse, roughly pulling them apart, he heard Kate moan. She was deepening the kiss, her hot, fierce attention making lust rage through his body like a desert storm, leaving no part of him untouched. His hands grazed over the lacy fabric of her bra to the swell of her breasts above, feeling the scatter of tiny goosebumps beneath his touch. Sliding her blouse over her shoulders, he let it fall to the floor behind her, and when Kate's fists knotted in his shirt he finally broke the kiss and took a step back so he could tug it over his head.

They stared at one another. Deliberately holding her gaze, Nikos slowly undid his belt buckle, then unfastened the buttons of his jeans one by one. Tugging them over his hips with hands that trembled in the effort of holding back, he impatiently kicked them to one side. Still holding her gaze, he stood before her, the might of his arousal straining against his boxers.

He wanted her so badly he thought he might scream with the power of it, but he could do this. He could make her wait. Just a bit longer.

Kate watched as Nikos slid his hand down inside his boxers. Her eyelids flickered, her throat moving on a swallow. Beneath the white cotton fabric his hand started to move, his eyes never leaving hers as he smoothly, steadily began to tease her, taunting her with this erotic show of sexual command.

Enough! Kate could stand it no longer. She wanted *her* hand around his magnificence. She wanted to feel him inside her. She wanted Nikos.

Tugging at the waistband of her leather trousers, she half fell, knocking her elbow against the corner of an ornately gilded chair when she tried to save herself. It hurt, but the frustration of trying to get the trousers off hurt far more.

Supressing a wail of frustration, she wriggled her way out of them as best she could, holding onto the edge of the chair to steady herself as she pulled at them with her other hand.

With a rush of movement Nikos was in front of her, lifting her effortlessly into the air before placing her back down in the chair. The offending trousers were peeled from her legs like a shed skin, taking her panties along with them. Then, pushing her thighs apart, Nikos knelt before her.

Kate gripped the arms of the chair. She was dimly aware of the sight of his dark head between her legs before she closed her eyes and surrendered herself to the utter bliss of his tongue. She moaned, long and deep, squirming so that the chair creaked beneath her, unable to stay still as the delirium inside her mounted with every sure lave of his tongue, every ecstatic touch.

Just as the first shudders of pleasure began to

surface she felt him move away, heard him stand up. Opening her eyes, she saw him stripping off his boxers. She held herself very still. Was he doing this deliberately to torture her?

She moved her hand down between her legs. She would finish this herself if she had to. With Nikos standing before her, looking like the epitome of every woman's wildest sexual fantasy, she could tip herself over the edge here and now without doing anything. Simply by gazing at the glorious sight of him.

'Uh-uh.' Reaching down, he removed her hand, placing it on her thigh. 'No, you don't. I've been waiting for this moment for far too long to be denied the final pleasure.'

Was that true? Had he really been waiting for her? For Kate, certainly, there had been no one else. What would have been the point? No man could ever match up to his strength and beauty, his potent virility. He was the very definition of alpha male, and when they had first met his sexy, confident ease had been the biggest turn-on, completely eliminating any virginal worries Kate might have had.

Now time and wealth had given that confidence a harder shell, polished it like armour, but the effect was just as lethal. His assured arrogance, his sheer perfection, still held Kate prisoner to his lure.

As he bent down to lift her off the chair Kate instinctively looped her arms around his neck. When her legs wrapped around his naked torso she pressed herself against him, nudging her sex against his groin, thrilling to the sensation of his hard body.

Nikos groaned deep in his throat. His mouth came down on hers, his kiss deep and wet as he took a step back, and then another, until Kate was pressed against the wall. There was a glorious second of anticipation before Nikos finally sank himself into her, long and hard and deep. Kate gasped, closing her eyes against the bliss of feeling him inside her, right up to the hilt, filling her so completely, so perfectly.

As he broke the kiss she heard his intake of breath.

'Open your eyes.'

It was a soft but deadly command. and as her lids opened Kate was immediately snared by the dark pool of his midnight gaze.

'That's better.'

Still asserting his authority, Nikos took total command. With their eyes locked together, he started to move. The first few strokes were slow, silky-smooth. With her back braced against the wall he had the control he wanted, moving his hips to get just the right angle, gripping her shoulders with each skilful thrust. But he needed more.

Uttering something low and deep in his native tongue, Nikos lifted her up and wrapped her legs around him again, transferring his hands to the wall on either side of her head.

He started to thrust. Harder, deeper, and deeper still, each stroke taking Kate nearer and nearer to the edge of that precipice of oblivion. She fought it for a long as she could, intent on prolonging the ecstasy, never wanting this exquisite pleasure to end. But as Nikos's thrusts became ever more forceful, his breath rasping hot and dry against her face, Kate gave herself permission to let go.

Her slick core tightened, then spasmed, and then again, building and building until Kate shook violently with the ultimate bliss, surrendering control to the ecstatic wonder of her orgasm, to the wonder of Nikos.

And as she fell she took Nikos with her. His

guttural moan echoed around the room, his jerky shudder of release resonating throughout her body, filling her with joy.

CHAPTER EIGHT

'WHAT TIME IS IT?'

Kate murmured the words against his naked chest.

'Hmm…not sure.'

With the shutters closed, the bedroom was so dark there was no way of knowing. They had been in his bed for hours, Nikos did know that. And still he felt a wave of desire kicking in again. He could never have enough of Kate. Sex with her now was just as amazing, just as perfect, as it had been the first time around. Kate knew how to turn him on in a way that no other woman ever had or ever could. Somehow they just fitted, anticipating each other's needs to perfection. Somehow it was just right.

And, judging by her moans of pleasure, by the wild thrashing of her limbs, the long, endless juddering of her beautiful orgasms, it felt the same for Kate. Nikos had made damned sure of it, in fact.

The thought that he might be compared to some other lover, past, present or future, filled him with a blind kind of fury that he couldn't even to begin to address. If he had his way, no other man would so much as touch a hair on her head, let alone take her to bed.

Which left them where, exactly?

Nikos had no idea. Neither did he want to examine it. Right now they were man and wife, in bed together, doing what came so very naturally to them. He was going to make the most of that.

'You hungry?'

Releasing his arm from where it was trapped under Kate's body, he smoothed his hand over the top of her head. He loved the feel of her hair when it was short like this, silky and springy beneath his touch. He loved the way he could rake his fingers through it, feeling her scalp beneath. He loved the way it tickled his skin when she dipped her head to kiss his body, to taste him, to take him in her mouth.

He wanted to do it all over again. And again. But his stomach was telling him he had other needs.

'Starving.'

'Good.'

He swung his legs over the bed, pulled on a pair of boxers and crossed the room to open the shutters. On the other side of the majestic Grand Canal the buildings were floodlit a soft gold, the cafés busy under their red awnings. A couple of illuminated pleasure boats cut through the inky water.

'Eat out or Room Service?'

He turned to look back at Kate, who had propped herself up in bed with the large pillows. With her face in shadow, he couldn't easily read her expression, but her voice was warm and soft.

'Room service, please.'

'Anything in particular that you fancy?' He stepped closer, just in time to see her bite back a smile.

'You choose.'

Walking through to the adjoining salon, Nikos phoned through his order, then looked around for his cell phone. Finding it still in the pocket of his discarded jeans, he brought the screen to life as he walked back into the bedroom. He could hear Kate in the bathroom, splashing water in the basin.

Getting back into bed, he started to look at his messages. It was nine-thirty in the evening here in Italy, but different time zones meant there was always something happening somewhere in the world that needed his attention. The Nikoladis empire comprised a wide range of different businesses and enterprises, employing several thousand people. It was a big responsibility, and Nikos knew he had a reputation for being a hard task manager. But you didn't succeed in business without being ruthless.

However, work held no interest for him tonight. This was all about enjoyment and making it last as long as he could. He didn't know what tomorrow held, and for the moment he didn't care.

However, one text message did catch his eye and he clicked to open it.

'Anything interesting?'

The mattress moved as Kate got into bed beside him, sliding a hand to his thigh. She was wearing a hotel robe and smelled of lemon soap.

'It's from Sofia.'

'Oh, right…'

Nikos heard the caution in Kate's voice, as if talking about Sofia was off limits.

'She says she's going on a school trip to London and she'd like to meet up there.'

'And will you?'

'*We* will, yes. You and me.'

'Nikos.' Kate took her hand away. 'Don't you think this is a bit unfair on Sofia? Fooling her like this…pretending that we're a happily married couple? I mean, the poor girl has been through enough, hasn't she? Without us letting her down as well.'

'I have no intention of letting her down. Quite the reverse. I am doing all this to protect her.'

'But…'

'Sofia knows the score, Kate. She knows that our marriage is simply a means to an end. That once the courts have granted me legal guardianship it will be dissolved.'

'Oh.'

Nikos watched as Kate bit down on her lip. If he didn't know better, he would have thought she looked hurt.

'And what does Sofia think about that?'

'She's cool with it.'

Kate hesitated. 'And what does she think about me?'

'I don't know.' Nikos frowned. 'I've never asked.'

'But what reason did you give her for me agreeing to go along with all this?'

'I told her you were doing it for the money.'

'Nikos!' Kate pulled away.

'Well, it's the truth, isn't it?'

'Well, yes, but...'

'So what's the problem? Sofia is smart and knowing and she's very independent for her age. She's had to be. I think you'll like her. Oh, good—food.'

At the sound of the knock on the door, Nikos leapt out of bed again. Kate watched his retreating form—the way the shadows played across the muscles of his back, the tapered waist, the strong, firm length of his bare legs. So perfect.

He was back in no time, wheeling a trolley laden with domed silver dishes.

'Where would *madame* like to take her evening meal?' With a flourish, he draped a white linen napkin over his arm and picked up the lift-off tray.

Kate smiled, pushing away the feeling of unease that had started to creep over her. She mustn't let herself spoil this precious evening with nagging doubt. She should be glad that Sofia had been told the truth—even if it did mean she would probably think Kate was a gold-digging little tramp. Perhaps she was...

'Here on the bed, please.' She held out her arms to take the tray from Nikos. He had made it look light as feather, but her arms almost buckled under the weight.

'You okay with it?'

'Sure.' She settled it down on the bedcovers.

Meanwhile Nikos was opening a bottle of champagne, expertly filling two flutes. Handing one to Kate, he got into bed beside her and held his glass aloft.

'To us.'

Kate clinked her glass against his. 'Yes, to us.' She took a sip, feeling the bubbles sliding down her throat. 'Whatever *us* is.'

She hadn't meant to say that. She knew the rules—why was she pretending that she didn't? Why would she want to challenge the status quo and expose herself to the certainty of being hurt?

'*Us* is we two, here and now, living for the moment.' Nikos took a large swallow of champagne.

Kate nodded. That would have to do. But deep inside her a small voice yearned for more.

The food was delicious and they both tucked in hungrily. Nikos had ordered far too much, but they attacked it with gusto, passing each other forkfuls of sea bass carpaccio and smoked salmon ravioli, exclaiming through full mouths about how good it was.

Finally stuffed, they leant back against the pillows, the wreckage of the meal still scattered on the bed before them.

'Thank you.' Kate turned to smile at Nikos, raising her hand to remove a crumb from his lip.

Nikos caught her hand and kissed it, his open mouth damp against her knuckles. 'You are very welcome, *agape mou*.' He emptied the last of the champagne into their glasses, holding up the bottle to look at it. 'Shall I get us another?'

'No.' Kate shook her head, laughing. 'Not unless you want to knock me out completely.'

'Trust me…' His eyes smouldered with intent. 'That's the last thing I want.'

The bottle was tossed to the floor as his arms went around her again, making the crockery and the silverware on the bed topple and crash together nosily.

'Wait!'

Kate extricated herself from his arms and set about clearing the bed, filling the tray and placing it back on the trolley. She could feel Nikos's eyes watching her every move, and when she turned to look at him, he patted the bed beside him.

'Get back into bed, woman.' It was an order, both playful and sexy.

Kate pressed her lips together. There was nothing she wanted to do more, but the worm of worry had reared its head again, and was refusing to be ignored.

Cautiously, she slid back in beside him. 'Thank you for bringing me here to Venice.' She arranged the sheet around her. 'It has been wonderful. An experience I will never forget.'

'I was hoping it would be.' A wicked smile twinkled his eyes. 'And it's not over yet.'

He rolled on his side, sliding his warm leg in between hers, his intentions clear.

Kate pulled away slightly. 'Nikos, don't you think we should talk?'

'Not really.' He nuzzled into her neck, nipping at the lobe of her ear. 'I can think of much better things to do.'

With a soft laugh Kate felt her eyelids start to close against his sensual assault—before reality crept in again. Pushing herself back against the pillows, she turned to look at him, gazing at the hard perfection of his body, the strikingly handsome planes of his shadowed face. And when he smiled at her, her heart whispered with longing.

'I mean it, Nikos.' She started to pleat the linen sheet beneath her fingers. 'This past week or so has been such a whirlwind—the whole marriage thing, all the travelling, and now this...' She flashed him a nervous glance.

'You regret making love with me?' His question was typically direct, his eyes dark, challenging.

'No.' Kate knew for certain that was true. How could she regret doing something that had felt so wonderful? So right. 'I don't regret it, Nikos. What about you?' A shot of fear tinged her voice.

'No.' He sat up, roughly arranging the pillows behind him. 'Me neither. Far from it.' His hand slid under the covers to rest on Kate's thigh, gently stroking away her fears. 'So, if it's not to admonish me for being a wicked seducer, what do you want to talk about?'

'I don't know.' Kate chewed down on her lip. 'Maybe you could tell me about Sofia. If I'm to meet her I'd like to learn more about her.'

'Sofia is funny and sassy and very bright. She's a great kid.'

Kate was surprised to see his eyes shining with something like pride. 'You two have got quite close then?'

'Yeah.' Nikos gave a small nod. 'I'd like to think so.'

Kate hesitated. 'Philippos's death must have come as a terrible shock to her.'

'*Fysika*. Of course.' Nikos removed his hand from her thigh and raked it through his ruffled hair, his jaw tightening.

'And for you too?'

'Yes, Kate, for me too.'

He gave a weary sigh, and for a moment Kate feared that the shutters were going to come down.

But then in a low voice he continued, 'It was hard to take in. It still is.'

'I'm sure.' Cautiously Kate felt for his hand, which had come to rest outside the covers, and softly laid her own over it. 'Did you have any idea that Philippos...that he was suffering from mental health problems?'

'Not really. I hadn't been back to Crete for some time. After we sold the software patent our business relationship was dissolved. We went our separate ways.'

'And what about Sofia? Did she know?'

'She was away at some fancy boarding school. Philippos obviously decided he had to do *some-*

thing with all that money he'd made.' Nikos's throat moved on a swallow. 'I thought I was doing the right thing, Kate. I thought that making Philippos rich and successful would make him happy. Instead I ruined his life.'

'Why would you *say* that?' Kate edged closer to him, squeezing his hand under hers.

'Because it's true.'

'No.' Suddenly she felt an overwhelming need to comfort him, to take away the hurt in his eyes. 'You can't blame yourself for Philippos's death.'

'Can't I?' Shrugging off her hand, Nikos roughly pulled back the sheet and got out of bed. 'You just watch me. If I hadn't gone back to Agia Loukia that summer, seen what Philippos was working on and persuaded him to let me market it commercially, his genius idea would have stayed on the drawing board. He would never have had to try and cope with the pressures of such unexpected wealth. He would still be alive. And Sofia would still have a brother.'

'You don't know that, Nikos.' Scooting across the bed, Kate jumped out too, the urge to rush and put her arms around him propelling her forward to where his proud figure was silhouetted against the window. 'Mental health problems are far more complicated to deal with than that.'

Nikos stilled, then turned to look at her, spearing her with his gaze. 'You sound like you speak from experience.'

She certainly did. Kate hesitated. In this moment of quiet she would have liked to tell him about her mother, but that would mean breaking her promise. So instead she sidestepped his remark. 'I know it's something a lot of people suffer from.'

'And there are all kinds of very effective treatments. If I had made time to see Philippos more often, found him some professional help, been the friend to him that I should have been, I know I could have saved him. But instead of that I was too busy making money, turning my own millions into billions. Scarcely giving a thought to how he was coping.'

'Punishing yourself now is not going to bring Philippos back, Nikos.' Kate pressed a hand to his chest, feeling the heartbeat beneath.

'I know that.' Nikos turned his head. 'Trust me, if it could I would willingly accept the harshest punishment going.'

Kate gazed at his noble profile, at his jaw held

tight with grief. Very gently she turned him to face her again. 'It's far better to channel that negative energy into something positive.' She gave him a tender smile. 'Taking care of Sofia, for example.'

'You are right.'

Nikos let out a pent-up breath. Gathering Kate's hand in his, he moved it down to her side, then ran his fingers the length of her arms. Kate's senses skittered with pleasure.

'Which is why I am determined to be there for Sofia in a way I never was for Philippos. I know I can never replace her brother, but I'm going to try my hardest to be the next best thing. I will do everything within my power to make sure she has the best life possible.'

'Even get married to a woman you despise?' The words escaped Kate's lips before she could stop them.

Nikos gave a soft huff. 'I have never despised you, Kate. Don't ever think that.' He laced his fingers through hers, drawing her against his naked chest and holding her close. 'I'll admit that my feelings for you over the years have been harsh. Our bitter break-up saw to that. But despise you? No—never. How could I when we can share something so special?'

Sex. He was talking about sex, that was all. But nuzzled against his muscled chest, breathing in his warm scent, Kate allowed herself to dream, just for this moment.

And when Nikos released one hand, leading her back towards the bed with the other, softly asking if she would stay with him tonight, she knew there was only one answer. She knew she was lost.

CHAPTER NINE

'HI.'

Kate looked up into the heavily kohled eyes of a pretty teenager.

'Hello, Sofia.' Getting to her feet, she stretched out her hand in greeting, but Sofia immediately pulled her into a hug. She smelled of some sort of exotic incense. 'I am so pleased to meet you.'

'You too,' said Sofia, looking around her, scanning the other diners in the smart restaurant.

'And Happy Birthday!'

'Thanks.'

'How does it feel to be sixteen?'

'Pretty much the same as fifteen.' Sofia sat down in the chair Nikos had pulled out for her and picked up the menu.

Kate laughed. To be fair it had been a pretty dumb question. She studied the teenager over the top of her menu. The first thing she'd noticed was her hair, shaved over one ear, it was dyed in shades of pink, green and blue, and artfully mussed so that it framed her pretty face like a spiky rainbow. She was wearing skinny jeans with rips all the way down and a skimpy black camisole top. Kate immediately liked her.

'What are you two going to have?' Nikos put down his menu. 'I understand the chateaubriand is very good.'

Kate gazed across at him, trying her hardest to control the silly smile that threatened to creep over her face whenever she looked at him. The last few days had been so lovely she felt like she was floating on a cloud. But clouds, as she had to keep reminding herself, could quickly disappear...

Continuing their grand tour, they had spent three days in Barcelona, visiting all the tourist spots and soaking up the culture.

And even though the paparazzi had been in attendance, snapping pictures of them gazing up in awe at the Sagrada Familia or wandering arm in arm down Las Ramblas, the bustling, tree-lined street in the centre of the city, this time it had been different. When they'd asked her to pose for the camera she hadn't felt like a fraud, as if it was all a gruesome pretence. This time her smile had been genuine. Her happiness real.

Like a switch being flicked, their relationship had completely altered since that night in Venice. Gone was the cold, harsh Nikos, who'd looked at her with such antipathy, treated her with such callous disregard. He had been replaced by a charming, attentive, funny and deeply sexy lover. The man she had fallen so madly in love with in Crete, in fact.

Except that wasn't quite true. Nikos had altered—they both had. He was a stronger, more powerful version of himself, and all the more compelling for that. Success had honed him, made him sharper, more astute. And the way he wore his wealth only heightened his allure.

He was unostentatiously generous—particularly with taxi drivers or hotel staff or waiters… people to whom it meant the most. Maybe he remembered what it was like to be a humble waiter himself. Either way, this new Nikos was a whole new heartbreaking force to be reckoned with.

This trip to London—the last on their honeymoon itinerary—had been timed so they could take Sofia out for her birthday. Kate had been nervous about meeting her, especially since finding out that Nikos had told Sofia she had married him for money. Kate could have done without that, even if it *was* the truth.

But if Sofia had any concerns about Kate and her motives they weren't showing. Instead she was screwing up her nose as she read the menu. 'D'you think I could have a burger?' She put the menu down. 'That's what I'd really like.'

'In that case, that's what you shall have,' Nikos said. 'It is your birthday after all. Kate? Have you decided?'

'Yes. I'll have a burger too, please.' She smiled at him.

'Three burgers it is, then.' Nikos signalled to the waiter.

'And don't forget the fries,' Sofia reminded him. 'Lots of them—I'm starving. And I'll have a double rum and Coke.'

'*Den tha!* You will *not*!'

'Okay. I guess I'll just have to make do with a glass of champagne, then.' She gave him a cheeky grin. 'So that we can all toast my birthday.'

With their orders taken, Nikos sat back in his chair, studying Sofia with his fingers steepled under his chin. Kate was fascinated to see the relationship between these two. It was obviously warm, and surprisingly close. Nikos hadn't been exaggerating when he'd said they'd got to know each other well. There was a genuine affection between them—a teasing banter such as true siblings might have.

Not that Kate had ever had the chance to experience such a thing. But this was a side of Nikos that Kate had never seen before. And she found herself strangely moved.

'And what, young lady, is *that*?' Nikos was pointing to the rather sore-looking piercing for a stud in Sofia's delicate nostril.

'Oh, that…' Sofia nonchalantly touched her nose. 'My birthday present to myself. I've wanted one for ages, but if you're under sixteen you have to have written confirmation from a parent or guardian, and as I'm only a ward of court at the moment I had to wait. What do you think?'

'I think…' Nikos put on a mock-stern voice '… that even if I had been your guardian I wouldn't have been signing forms allowing you to mutilate your body.'

Sofia rolled her eyes. 'Honestly, Nikos, when did you turn into such an old grouch?'

Kate bit back a smile at the teenager's taunting.

'I bet *you* have piercings, don't you, Kate?' She picked up a piece of bread and tore off a chunk.

'No—well, only my ears.'

Suddenly Kate wished that she was riddled with piercings, so she could show her cool credentials to Sofia. But the fact was she would never have been allowed to have her nose pierced, or her head shaved, or even wear ripped jeans, like the lively teenager before her. Kate's mother had ruled supreme when it had come to her appearance, and had still been picking out her dresses for her when Kate had been in her late teens.

All in the name of Kandy Kate, of course, to preserve its squeaky clean image. Even when she had escaped to university she had been warned by Fiona that she must dress 'appropriately' at all times, and never forget who she was.

'Shame. You would suit something dramatic with your hairstyle. A stud above your lip, maybe, or at least a helix piercing. That's here...' she leant across to touch Kate's ear '...in the cartilage at the top.'

'I'll bear that in mind.' Kate smiled. 'Maybe I'll do just that. What do you think, Nikos?'

'I think I like your ears just as they are.' Nikos

gave her a solemn stare before looking down, as if he had somehow given himself away. But Kate felt herself glow with pleasure.

'Your hair is cool, by the way.' Sofia chattered on.

'Thank you.' All these compliments could turn a girl's head. 'I like yours too.'

'Oh, look—here comes the champagne.'

The meal carried on happily, with Sofia keeping them entertained and making their table by far the most lively in this rather stuffy establishment. Kate wouldn't have chosen this place, she thought. She would have picked a more modern place—somewhere more edgy. Although she had to admit that the burgers were good.

'So, where have you two visited so far?' Sofia wiped her mouth with her napkin and picked up another handful of fries.

'We started in Paris, then Rome, Venice and Barcelona.' Nikos ran through their itinerary. 'London is our last stop.'

'Cool. And which place did you like best?'

'I would say Venice—or maybe Barcelona.' Nikos caught Kate in his dark gaze again. 'How about you, Kate?

Stupidly, Kate felt herself blush. 'Yes, both those places were a lot of fun.'

'Indeed.'

Nikos's low voice caught Sofia's attention and her eyes travelled from one of them to the other, taking everything in as she slowly licked her fingers.

'Are you not going to Greece, Nikos? Surely you want to show Kate Athens?'

'Kate has already visited the Acropolis.'

That was true. It had been her first stop on her solo trip to Europe, which felt like a lifetime ago now.

'I don't mean the Acropolis—I mean the *real* Athens, where the fun stuff is. I tell you what, Kate…' Sofia warmed to her theme '…you and I should go together. I have loads of friends there. We would have a blast.'

'Thank you.' Kate touched Sofia's hand, looking down at the chunky silver rings on her slender fingers. 'That would be lovely.'

If extremely unlikely. Much as she liked this engaging young woman, she knew she would never be part of her life. As soon as Nikos became her legal guardian he and Kate would divorce and she would never see her again. Which was a shame.

'How's the legal stuff going, anyway?' Sofia lifted the bottle of champagne out of the ice bucket and, seeing it was empty, waved it at Nikos. 'Shall we get another one?'

'I think one bottle is enough.' Nikos frowned at her. 'And, in answer to your question, it's going slowly. There are few things I want to discuss with you.'

'Please speak Greek if you want to.' Kate interjected. 'Don't feel you have to use English because of me.'

'Of course we will speak English,' Sofia replied. 'It would be rude not to. And besides, I want Nikos to see all the money spent on my education hasn't been wasted.'

Kate laughed. 'Your English is great!'

As the two of them started talking Kate excused herself to go to the bathroom. She felt as if she was eavesdropping on something that was really none of her business. It also highlighted her part in this charade—the fact that she had only married Nikos for money. And that made her feel horribly awkward.

She took her time, and when she returned Nikos was asking for the bill.

'Ah, Kate, I was just going to give Sofia her present.'

'Ooh, thanks!' Sofia's face lit up with child-like expectation, and suddenly Kate realised how young she really was.

'Here.' Nikos passed her a blue velvet box. 'I hope you like it. Kate helped me choose.'

Kate chewed her lip nervously. When she and Nikos had visited the exclusive jewellers before lunch, the gold charm bracelet had seemed like a most suitable gift. Now she had met Sofia she could see it was all wrong.

Sofia opened the hinged box with a squeak and Kate's brow furrowed with unease.

'I *love* it!' Sofia was on her feet in a moment, flinging her arms around Nikos first and then Kate. 'Thank you so much.'

Kate gave her a hug. It was a great performance. What a lovely girl she was.

She waited until Nikos had gone to find them a cab before taking Sofia to one side. 'You can always swap that bracelet for something else. Like a few hundred nose rings.'

Sofia laughed, linking arms with Kate as they

stepped out onto the busy sidewalk. 'I would never do that. True, it's not the sort of thing that I would normally wear, but Nikos bought it for me, and for that reason alone I will treasure it.'

Kate could see she was telling the truth. She could see how much Nikos meant to her, how fond she was of him. And for some reason that made her feel even worse.

It was Sofia's idea to go to a pub. With several hours before she had to re-join her classmates, back at the hotel, Nikos had suggested some touristy things that they might do: The Tower of London, the London Eye, the British Museum… But Sofia had politely declined, saying that what she really wanted was to find a traditional old English pub—like the ones in the rom com movies she and her friends watched when they should be doing their homework.

It had seemed an innocent enough request, and after emphasising that she would only be allowed soft drinks Nikos had led them to a little pub called The Nag's Head.

Sofia immediately lit up with excitement. It was dingy inside, and smelled of stale ale, but Kate had to admit the place had a certain charm.

With dark red walls and a wooden floor, it had small cast iron tables and a curved bar, with pewter tankards hanging above it like the ghostly relics of drinkers past.

Insisting that she wanted to sit at the bar, so she could see what was going on, Sofia was thrilled to discover she could legally have a glass of shandy, and watched with rapt attention as the barman picked up a dimpled half pint mug, filled it half-full with beer from a polished brass beer pump, and topped it up with lemonade.

Raising it to her lips, Sofia declared it 'delicious', but she was still nursing the same glass an hour later. By which time Nikos was getting twitchy.

'We should be thinking about going.'

'Aw, not yet.' Sofia tugged her phone out of her jean's pocket to check the time. 'I don't need to be back for another hour at least.'

'I'm afraid I have some business to attend to before trading closes in New York.' Nikos was already shrugging on his jacket.

'Well, Kate will stay with me—won't you Kate? She'll make sure I get back to the hotel safely.'

'Yes, of course.'

Kate agreed willingly. She had been secretly hoping to spend some time alone with Sofia, so she could try to explain to her why she had agreed to this fake marriage. Tell her how she intended to pay the money back—every cent—when Kandy Kate was thriving again.

Nikos hesitated, looking from one of them to the other doubtfully. But Sofia had a way of winning him round, and after issuing strict instructions about not being late and taking taxi cabs and sticking together at all times, he finally left.

Everything started well enough. Broaching the subject of her arrangement with Nikos, Kate was surprised to find that Sofia, far from criticising her for being a mercenary tramp, was actually *grateful* to her, thanking her profusely for marrying Nikos and so upping the chances of Nikos becoming her guardian.

It occurred to Kate that, despite what Nikos had told her, Sofia didn't know about the money. She thought Kate was doing it out of the kindness of her heart. But there was nothing to be gained by explaining the situation fully, so Kate dropped the subject, her guilt soothed slightly by the fact that Nikos must have cared enough to want to protect her image.

Instead they talked about Philippos. Full of pride, Sofia related what a genius he'd been, how much he'd valued his friendship with Nikos, how he had been the best brother in the world. Her large eyes filled with tears as she talked about his tragic death, all but breaking Kate's heart. Pulling her into a hug, Kate held her tight, wishing she could do more.

But Sofia quickly recovered. Giving a couple of sniffs, she tipped up her chin and offered her a watery smile. 'But, hey, this is my birthday. So I refuse to be sad.'

The pub was starting to get much busier, and the clientele now were a different, noisier crowd. The old men playing dominoes in the corner had gone, to be replaced by smart City types, all striped shirts and red braces, flashing their platinum credit cards.

And Sofia was loving it. When a group of persistent young men found out it was her birthday they insisted on buying her and Kate a drink, and Sofia accepted before Kate could stop her, swapping her shandy for a mocktail and ordering a mojito for Kate.

Kate had no interest in these flashy City guys, with their fat wallets and their narrow, unchallenged views, vying to impress these two foreigners. But Sofia was having such a good time. And with all the sorrow she had had in her life Kate thought she deserved a bit of light-hearted fun. So, not wanting to play the meanie, she sipped her drink and stayed quiet as the banter continued.

She only left her charge for five minutes, giving Sofia strict instructions to stay exactly where she was. But, to Kate's utter horror, when she returned from the bathroom Sofia had gone.

In a state of blind panic Kate rushed out into the street, scanning in every direction, desperately trying to catch a glimpse of that multi-coloured hair. There was no sign of her. Running back into the pub, she dashed through to the beer garden, with the image of Nikos's livid face emblazoned on her brain.

He would never forgive her if anything had happened to Sofia. And she would never forgive herself.

And then she saw her, backed up against the garden trellis, with one of the City guys pressing himself close against her. *Way too close.*

Without thinking, Kate stormed towards them, wrenching the man's arm from where his hand was hooked in the trellis just above Sofia's head and forcibly pushing him away. There was the sound of splintered wood, an indignant yell from the man, and a sort of yelp of surprise from Sofia as the trellis came away from the wall and a tangle of plants and wood fell around them.

'What the hell do you think you're doing?' The man stepped away, stumbling over the debris and glaring at Kate.

'Are you okay, Sofia?' Kate put a protective arm around her shoulders.

Sofia nodded. 'Yeah, of course. I can take care of myself, you know.' But Kate could see her cheeks were flushed, her eyes wide.

'And *you…*' Kate rounded on the man, who was picking bits of leaf off his suit. 'You should know better. You keep your dirty hands off my… my…' *Stepdaughter? Friend?* Kate was at a loss to know how to describe her. The truth was far too complicated. 'Off Sofia.'

'Chill, lady…' The guy moved closer. 'There's no need to get so worked up. To be honest, you're far more my type anyway.'

'Get lost.'

Kate went to brush past him, but he took a step to the side, blocking her path.

'Aw, don't be like that...'

'Get out of my way.'

'Make me.'

She didn't need telling twice.

Putting her palms flat against his chest, Kate pushed hard—but the guy grabbed hold of her wrists. Sofia leapt to her rescue, rushing at him from the side and sending a swift, hard kick to his shins. The man swore violently as his legs buckled beneath him and he fell to the ground, taking Kate with him.

They ended up in a jumble of limbs, the man flat on his back with Kate sprawled on top of him. As a small crowd formed around them, jeering and laughing, Kate hurriedly got to her feet. With as much dignity as she could muster, she pushed her way through. Reaching for Sofia's hand, she marched the two of them out of the beer garden, through the pub and onto the pavement outside.

As they stood waiting for a black cab, Kate's breath still rasping in her chest, she turned to address the birthday girl. 'Sofia, I think it's probably best if we don't mention what just happened there to Nikos.'

Sofia laughed, removing a bit of greenery from

Kate's hair and letting it drop to the ground. 'You're not kidding! He would go *ballistic*!'

'So it's our secret, then, yes?' Sofia's colourful assessment of Nikos's likely reaction did nothing to make Kate feel better.

'Definitely our secret.' Sofia linked her arm through hers, her eyes shining. 'And thanks, Kate.' She gave her a kiss on the cheek. 'This has been the best birthday *ever*!'

CHAPTER TEN

NIKOS STOOD WITH his hands on his hips, staring at the panoramic view of London. From up here, in this office on the seventy-second floor of the Shard, it was certainly an impressive vista, with the famous London landmarks all there, and the snaking brown water of the River Thames far below.

Impatient, he checked his watch again. He was early, but he wanted to get this meeting over with.

Returning to his seat, he took another sip of his coffee, putting down the cup with his lip curled in distaste. Suddenly he wanted to be back in Crete, in his own immaculate white villa, enjoying a cup of proper Greek coffee, with nothing to worry about except where he was going to take his boat out that day and how many fish he might catch.

Who was he kidding? When was the last time he'd been fishing? He couldn't even remember.

That life was long gone, together with the happy-go-lucky guy Nikos had once been.

Breaking up with Kate had been the catalyst—completely changing the course of his life. Before then he had skimmed through life like a pebble across the water, never bothering to ask himself if he was happy. Never going that deep. Because he hadn't been sure he'd like what he found.

He'd had his wits, his looks and his charm—and he had believed that had been more than enough to ease his passage through life and provide him with an endless supply of beautiful women to grace his arm and his bed. He had done his stint in the army, proud to serve his country, and he had travelled the world with little more than a battered rucksack and a handful of the local currency. Money, he had convinced himself, was of little importance.

Returning to Agia Loukia on the orders of his father had not been part of his plan—not that he'd ever *had* much of a plan—but in some ways it had been good to be home. He'd almost forgotten the perfect blue of the Cretan sky, the beauty of the sunset over the water. His father had been as difficult as ever, but Nikos had learnt how to handle him—and anyway, it was only to be a temporary arrangement.

At the start of that summer he'd had no inkling that his life was about to change so irrevocably— first by going into business with Philippos and then by falling in love with Kate O'Connor.

Even to this day Nikos still wasn't sure how the latter had happened. With his parents' doomed relationship as his only role model, he had vowed he was never going to let himself get involved. Never going to trust a woman.

Somewhere buried deep in his subconscious he had been dimly aware that being rejected by his mother at such a young age had coloured his whole view of the female race. Not for him the rosy-pink glow of romance—more a sort of no-nonsense beige. He'd always taken great pleasure in the company of women, but that was as far as it went.

Until Kate. Meeting Kate had blown all his cast-iron resolutions out of the water. Before he'd known it he, the hardened bachelor, the die-hard sceptic, had found himself down on one knee, slipping a handmade silver ring onto Kate's finger, declaring his undying love.

He remembered that day with such vivid clarity. The two of them so happy…sitting on the beach side by side, watching the sun set. Then going back to his little white cottage with the blue shutters and the baby lizards running across the walls. Making love all night long. They had been different people then. Living in a different world.

Afterwards work had been both his salvation and his nemesis. Using it to block out the pain, he had worked all hours, pushing himself to the limits of endurance and beyond. Marketing and then selling Philippos's brilliant idea had earned them both a fortune. But what good had it done them? Nikos had become a bigshot businessman, his only aim in life to make more and more money—money he didn't need or even want. Money had turned him into a man he didn't recognise. Or even like. And Philippos was dead… Something that Nikos would hold himself responsible for as long as he lived.

But recently, at least, he had been putting his money to good use. This morning he had received an update from his lawyers, telling him that his guardianship application was progressing favourably. Securing himself a wife—effectively buying Kate O'Connor—had been an excellent idea. As far as the lawyers were concerned anyway.

From his point of view it was more complicated.

A lot more complicated.

His conflicting feelings towards Kate had kept him awake last night. Somehow the acrimony he had felt towards her just a couple of weeks ago had gone, to be insidiously replaced by respect, admiration, affection. They worried him, these feelings—the way they could creep over him at any given moment, triggered by nothing more dramatic than a glance in her direction when she stopped to stroke a stray cat or smile at a toddler. They gave Kate a hold over him. And that was something Nikos needed to avoid at all costs.

He leant back into the sofa, telling himself to relax. Spending time with Sofia yesterday had been good. It had given him cause for hope. Seeing what a confident young woman she was growing into had thawed a little of the guilt he felt so deeply. Maybe the change in him these past three years hadn't been all bad. He realised he was ready for responsibility now, actively looking forward to taking on the challenge of a teenage girl. And he suspected Sofia would be quite a challenge!

She and Kate, of course, had hit it off like a house on fire. Watching them interact, listening to their conversation, he had felt a strange sense of pleasure creeping over him. He didn't know where it had come from, or why it had been there, but where Kate was concerned he never knew *what* to feel.

All he did know was that being around her rocked his very foundations. Desires that he'd buried deep within him, never to be revisited, had surfaced in a flood of craving and lust and desperate hunger that he now knew would never be sated.

The past few days bore testament to that. What had happened in Venice—finally taking Kate to his bed—had been meant to be a one-off. Nikos had been sure that sex with Kate would serve a purpose, settle an old score, and allow him to move on. *Slake his thirst.*

Except this particular thirst refused to be slaked. Instead he had found his craving increasing day on day, hour upon hour, until the 'one-off' had become two, three, four times. Until spending every night with her seemed perfectly natural. Inevitable. Imperative.

Up until last night, that was.

Having been immersed in work for a couple of hours, Nikos hadn't noticed the time to start with. But it hadn't been long before he'd found himself clock-watching, wondering when Kate would be back. *Looking forward to seeing her again.*

He'd told himself that he just wanted to make sure that Sofia had been safely returned to her school party, but in reality he'd known it wasn't that. Kate had got to him. No matter how much he fought against it, somehow she had insidiously wound her way around his heart. And that was deeply troubling.

When Kate had finally swept into their hotel suite Nikos had known immediately that something was wrong. His enquiry about whether they'd had a good time had been answered curtly, and Kate's reassurance that Sofia had been delivered back to her hotel had been uncharacteristically brusque.

There had been no mistaking her change of mood—especially when Kate had announced that she was very tired and taken herself off to her own room without even meeting his eye. Nikos had been left staring at her closed bedroom door, with the thrum of blood in his ears, wondering what on earth that had all been about. And, more importantly, why he cared? How the hell did she manage to have such an effect on him?

Much to his irritation, he'd found himself still mulling over the events of last night the next morning. Logic told him that a cooling in relations between them was a *good* thing. If Kate was making a tactical withdrawal he should be doing the same thing. This was the reality check he needed.

Their enforced honeymoon was almost at an end. It had served its purpose. Nikos had made sure they'd been seen together pretty much wherever they went, and posed photos of 'the happy couple' were gracing the gossip columns both here in Europe and in the US. It was all good PR for him, and Kandy Kate was benefitting too. Kate's marriage to a billionaire Greek tycoon had already seen the company's share price shoot up.

But logic refused to explain why Kate's rejection stuck like a fishhook in his skin. Why the more he tried to ignore it, the more it dug into him. If he didn't know better, he would say he was becoming infatuated with Kate O'Connor Nikoladis. And *that* was something he needed to avoid at all costs.

Nikos stood up again, pacing up and down in front of the wall of windows. He needed to put some space between them, that was all. There was no reason why they shouldn't be able to go their separate ways for a while now—they both had businesses to run, after all. The Greek courts couldn't expect them to be together *all* the time. At a later date, he would fly Kate out to Crete and then, with her by his side, he would make an appointment to see the clerk of the court and find out how his guardianship application was progressing.

But not yet. Right now he needed space to think.

Nikos checked his watch again. *Where was she?* He had gone to some considerable trouble to set up this meeting with the CEO of a leading confectionery company here in the UK. He'd been looking forward to telling Kate, seeing the surprise on her face. Okay, it wasn't the most romantic of gestures, but potentially this could mean a huge deal for Kandy Kate.

But as it turned out he hadn't had the chance to tell her anything before she'd taken herself off to bed. So he'd ended up sending her a text message, telling her to meet him at Rosebury's head office in the Shard at ten o'clock. As Nikos had pressed 'send' he'd told himself this would be his final involvement in Kate's business. After this she was on her own.

Leaning forward, he picked up one of the newspapers that were neatly lined up on the table—one of the red tops. It wasn't his usual sort of reading material, but he was just killing time. After flipping through the pages of scaremongering politics and salacious gossip about footballers' wives, he was just about to toss it back on the table when a headline caught his eye.

Wrenching the page open, he stared at it in abject horror.

Randy Kate! the headline screamed at him. And below there was a photograph of Kate, sprawled on top of a man on the ground. *What the hell?* And, if that wasn't bad enough, amongst the group of people surrounding them there was

Sofia, looking down on them with a panicked expression on her face.

With shaking hands, Nikos scanned the article below.

Caught frolicking in a London beer garden yesterday evening, newlywed Kate Nikoladis, recently married to wealthy Greek businessman Nikos Nikoladis, seemed to be enjoying some downtime with an unknown admirer.

Heiress to the Kandy Kate confectionery business, Kate may be the nation's sweetheart in the US, but will this lead to a sticky situation with her heart-throb husband?

'Hi.'

He heard Kate approaching behind him.

'Not late, am I?'

Nikos turned slowly, not trusting himself to speak for a second as rage coursed through him, hot and fierce.

'What...' finally finding a modicum of control, he held up the open newspaper, shaking it in front of her '...is the meaning of *this*?'

Kate took the paper from him, her face draining of colour as she quickly scanned the article.

'Oh, hell.' She dropped it onto the table.

'*Well?*' Nikos's voice shook with anger.

'Look, there was a bit of an incident in the beer garden after you left last night.'

'Go on.'

'This guy came on to Sofia…'

'He did *what*?' The heat of his rage intensified.

'I intervened, and we got into a bit of a scrap, and—'

'A *scrap*? Is that what you call *this*?' Nikos gestured furiously to the photograph.

'It was something and nothing, Nikos. I dealt with it.'

'And this is your way of *dealing* with it is, is it? Throwing yourself on top of a total stranger and showing yourself up in front of everyone? In front of Sofia?'

Stunned into silence, Kate could only stare at Nikos, her heart thumping harder with every passing second. Okay, she'd messed up, but Nikos was overreacting. She had expected him to be annoyed—angry, even—but not to turn it into a personal attack. Everything they had shared in the last few days together—the pleasure, the intimacy, the sense of really getting to know one another—had instantly vanished, obliterated by the cold rage in Nikos's eyes.

But then, standing there, unable to move, Kate felt her initial surprise harden into something colder, like a fist closing round her heart. It was Nikos's use of the phrase 'showing yourself up'—a phrase she had heard all too often in her childhood and her teens, thrown at her by her mother whenever Kate had a smudge on her nose or a hole in her tights or wasn't looking one hundred percent picture-perfect.

And Nikos was just the same, wasn't he? Just as bad. Despite what Kate wanted to believe— what her poor battered heart so wanted to be true—Nikos was using her in the same way as her mother had used her. Like a commodity, a possession, to be paraded around when necessary, to look pretty, smile nicely, and keep her mouth shut. And when she made a mistake his default position was to punish her. Just like her mother.

Nikos had been controlling her from the very start of this ill-fated arrangement. Even during the meetings he had set up for Kandy Kate he had been the one doing the talking, the negotiating—as if Kate was little more than a cardboard cut-out. And she had let him. Because Nikos was a super-successful businessman and she couldn't even keep her family business afloat. Because Nikos was a hugely powerful, charismatic character.

No doubt he had been controlling her in Venice, and then in Barcelona too, when he had taken her to his bed. And Kate had fallen willingly into his arms, thrown herself headlong into his dark trap of seduction. Blinded by the power and passion of their lovemaking, Kate had allowed herself to imagine it as so much more, entertaining ridiculous fantasies of rekindling their relationship for real. Falling in love all over again. Now she saw that for Nikos it had just been sex.

Firming her quivering lip, Kate pushed back her shoulders, refusing to show her hurt. Her eyes strayed to the wretched photograph, taunting her. She had to admit she could see how it might be construed. The man's legs were splayed, and Kate had somehow managed to fall in between them, her dress riding up to her thighs. But *she* hadn't done anything wrong—that was the point.

'For your information, I did *not* throw myself on top of that man.' She firmed her lips. 'I was pushing him away from me and we tripped and fell. That's all.'

'And when exactly were you going to tell me about this?'

'I wasn't,' Kate replied hotly. 'And, considering the way you've just reacted like a chest-beating caveman, who can blame me?'

'And how do you *expect* me to react?' On his feet now, Nikos closed the space between them with a single lethal stride. 'When I open the paper and see this sort of filth staring back at me?'

Kate took in a breath, willing herself to stay calm, not to let him get to her. 'I've told you what happened. I am not going to explain myself any more.'

'Well, that's fine.' Nikos glared at her. 'Because I don't want to hear any more. I leave you in charge of Sofia for a couple of hours and *this* is the result. You do realise you've jeopardised everything I have been trying to achieve? Undone everything we have been working towards? Once the Greek press get hold of this—if they haven't already—it might well affect the court's decision.'

'Surely not?' Kate's fingers fiddled anxiously with the gold stud in her ear.

'My new bride draped between the legs of a

stranger while the minor I'm trying to become guardian of looks on in horror? What do you *think*, Kate?'

'I will explain. Go and speak to the court in person—make them see it was all a misunderstanding.'

'It's way too late for that, Kate. The damage is done.'

'No… It can't be…'

'Excuse me.' A door opened and the clipped English tones of a polished PA interrupted their fight. 'Mr Lewis will see you now.'

'One minute!' Nikos rapped over his shoulder.

'Of course…' With a look of surprise, the PA retreated.

'We'd better go in.' Kate drew in a ragged breath.

'Still thinking about your precious business, Kate?'

Nikos threw the words at her with such vicious scorn that Kate flinched.

'*You* set up this meeting, Nikos, not me. I don't want to keep Charles Lewis waiting. That would be very bad manners.'

'Then by all means go ahead.' Nikos stepped out of her way. 'Don't let me stop you.'

'You...you aren't coming in with me?'

'No, Kate, I am not. Do you *really* think I can sit beside you as your husband when you're plastered all over the papers like *that*?' He jabbed a finger in the direction of the newspaper.

'Mr Lewis won't be interested in my private life. He probably hasn't even seen the paper.'

'But *I* have, Kate, and that's enough.'

'Very well.' Kate pulled on a cloak of defiance. 'I will go in alone.'

'Yes, you do that Kate. I'll see you back at the hotel this evening.' He glowered at her, his lip thinning with hostility. 'On second thoughts, don't wait up. I may be late back.'

CHAPTER ELEVEN

IT WAS GONE midnight when Nikos finally returned to the hotel. Channelling his frustration into work, he had rented an office in the Shard for the day and fired off emails, demanded to see business reports, chased up contracts and negotiated new deals as if his life depended on it. Or his sanity.

Maybe it did. It wouldn't be the first time he had used work as his salvation.

To some extent, it had served its purpose. With his brain engaged in the complex legalities of negotiating a new deal or monitoring the figures on a volatile stock market, he had successfully managed to blot Kate out. But the second he'd stopped—the second he'd picked up his coffee cup and stared out of the window at the city of London—he'd found himself right back in Kate's thrall, his mind whirring with a surge of thoughts and conflicting emotions. None of which he wanted to examine.

As he let himself into their suite of rooms Nikos was determined that tonight was going to be a Kate-free zone—both mentally and physically. He would pour himself a drink, go to bed—*alone*—and get some sleep.

The place was in darkness, but as Nikos flicked on the light switch in the living room he saw with a stab of frustration that he wasn't alone. Kate was uncurling herself from the sofa, blinking against the light.

'Hi…'

'You still up?' He strode over to the sideboard, deliberately not meeting her eye.

'Yes. I wanted to talk to you before you go to bed.'

Before *you* go to bed. Not *we*. Taking the stopper out of the cut-glass decanter, Nikos noisily sloshed himself a generous measure of whisky. Clearly Kate was planning on sleeping alone too.

'What about?'

He turned, facing her now. She was wearing grey leisure pants and a white tee shirt. Her pale face was free from make-up and her hair was mussed on one side from where she had been resting against a cushion. She still looked gorgeous.

'Well, firstly I wanted to thank you properly for setting up that meeting with Rosebury's. It was very helpful.'

'And secondly?'

Nikos went to stand before her, towering over her. He didn't want her thanks for some stupid business deal. He wanted her to stand up and kiss him, long and hard and deep, and take away the torment in his head. He wanted her in his bed. Or out of his life.

He didn't know what the hell he wanted.

But his harsh tones had hit home. Nikos watched as Kate drew up her legs, defensively wrapping her arms around her knees.

'Secondly, I think we need to talk about us.'

'*Us?*' Nikos repeated the word with cruel contempt, the kick of whisky sharpening his tongue. 'There is no *"us".*'

A flicker of hurt crossed Kate's face but she recovered quickly, meeting his gaze full-on.

'Yes, there is, Nikos.' Her voice was soft, weary. 'Whether you like it or not, we *do* have a past, and we are tied together for the foreseeable future. And just recently...' she faltered, searching for the right words '...we have been intimate.'

'And which of those things would you like to talk about, Kate?' Nikos closed his fingers around the glass in his hand.

Kate stared at him, willing herself to stay strong. She didn't want to do any of this. Returning to the hotel hours ago, she had paced around in turmoil, not knowing what to do with herself. Instinct had told her to flee, to get away before Nikos could hurt her any more, break her heart still further. She had even packed her suitcase, looked up flights online.

But then she had stopped. Running away wasn't going to solve anything. If she was ever to be free of the hold Nikos had over her, ever to find any sort of closure, she had to face up to her demons. She had to face up to Nikos. No matter how hard it was to do. No matter how much it hurt.

'The past.' Kate took in a shuddering breath. 'The night we broke up. We have never discussed that.'

'What's to discuss?' Animosity emanated from Nikos in pulsing waves. 'You made it quite clear that you didn't want me there. That our so-called engagement had been hidden like a dirty secret. That I wasn't deserving of your love.'

'No.' Quietly Kate got to her feet, her voice little more than a whisper. 'That's not true. Please don't ever think that.'

'Then how do you explain your behaviour? Why you were so delighted to find out you weren't pregnant?'

'Because the timing was all wrong.' She came to stand before him. 'Daddy had just died and Mom needed my support. I knew I was going to have to take on the running of Kandy Kate. Everything was in chaos. Surely you can see that?' Exasperated, she ran a hand through her hair. 'To be honest, I thought you would be relieved too.'

'Then you thought wrong.'

Kate's eyelids closed as a bruised silence settled around them. She could feel her heart battling against the misery of what they had lost. *What might have been.*

'Then I apologise.' She made herself look up and meet his eyes again. 'I promise you it was never my intention to undermine you or offend you in any way.'

Nikos gave a low, dismissive growl. 'Well, either way it doesn't matter. Ultimately you did me a favour. Thanks to you I finally grew up.

I learnt the importance of money. How wealth gives you power and respect.'

'But money was never my driving force, Nikos.'

'No? Well, what are you doing here, then?' A sneer curled his lip. 'You'll be telling me next that you married me for *love*.'

Kate flushed. She felt as if Nikos was nailing down her coffin with one brutally timed blow after another.

'No.' The wretched flush deepened. 'I'm here to save Kandy Kate, as you well know. But not because of the money. I'm doing it for my father. Because Kandy Kate is all I have left of him.'

'Yeah…' Nikos folded his arms across his chest. 'So you keep saying.'

'Because it's *true*.' Kate's voice quavered, but a sudden need to make Nikos see she wasn't some mercenary, cold-hearted shrew drove her on. 'Far from condemning your lack of wealth, I was envious of the life you had when we first met. The freedom you had…the chance to build your own future from scratch.'

Nikos scoffed. 'But that envy soon wore off, didn't it, Kate? By the time I got to New York my so-called "freedom" looked dangerously close to poverty. And as for building my own life from scratch—why would you choose to do that when you were already at the top? I'm sure the gutter looked a long, long way down from the top of KK Towers.'

'You were *never* in the gutter, Nikos!'

'You and your mother treated me as if I was.'

'Don't exaggerate.' Kate frantically summoned all her fight to try and counter his onslaught. 'I admit I could have handled the situation better... forewarned my mother about who you were...'

'Forewarned?' Nikos threw the word back at her in disgust, his breath hot on her face, his eyes glittering with temper. 'That says it all, doesn't it? The fact that you had to *forewarn* your mother about me. Have you any idea how insulting that is?'

'I didn't mean it like that.'

Kate looked down at the ground. She was making everything worse.

With a silent apology to her mother, she drew in a quick breath. 'There are things about my mother I have never told you, Nikos. She's vulnerable. *Very* vulnerable. That's why I had to try so hard to keep the peace.'

'Save it, Kate. This isn't about your mother.'

Kate felt her uncomfortable confession tossed to one side as if nothing.

'This is about you and me. When I arrived in New York I thought we were equals, lovers— destined to share our lives together. I soon found out how wrong I was.'

'No, you weren't wrong. I thought the same.'

Kate reached out to him, her eyes beseeching, but Nikos caught hold of her hand and brought it down to his side.

'Well, you had a funny way of showing it.' Anger and heat pulsed in his voice before he collected himself. 'But what's done is done. And maybe you were right. Maybe I *didn't* have anything to offer you back then. I admit that I come from a humble background and, yes, my childhood was chaotic. When your mother walks out on you and your father can't cope life gets tough. There was no money, no stability, and sometimes no food—let alone a table to eat it off. But despite that I survived. Not only survived, but triumphed. I have succeeded where others have failed. Become richer and more successful than most people could even dream about. Now I can hold my head high, mix with A-list celebrities, royalty—the highest in the land. Now, thanks to *you*, Kate, no one will ever look down on me again.'

His throat moved as he swallowed hard, but when Kate looked away he put his hands on her shoulders, turning her so there was no escape from the burn of his eyes.

'Perhaps you should take a bow.'

'And perhaps *you* should take a long, hard look at who you have become.'

'Ha!' Nikos took away his hands but stayed intimately close, glaring down at her from his towering height. 'That's rich, coming from you. Have you forgotten where I found you, *agape mou*? Dressed like a hooker and sprawled across the lap of a sweaty banker.'

'Have *you* forgotten how sometimes you have to do something you'd rather not do just to pay the bills?' Kate desperately tried to beat back his merciless assault.

'No, I've not forgotten.' Nikos's brows met in a scowl. 'How could I forget when you've just confirmed that the only reason you are here is to save your precious business. You are *still* doing something you would rather not do, aren't you, Kate? You can dress it up however you like— present it as an homage to your father if it makes you feel better—but you are *still* using my money for your own gain. You are effectively still *just paying the bills.*'

Kate blinked hard against his bitter words. Nikos had no right to hurl such accusations at her when they were both in the same boat. They were both using each other for their own gain. But what was the point of arguing? What could she say, anyway, that wouldn't either confirm that he was right or, far worse, betray what he really meant to her?

'So are we done talking?' With a note of triumph, Nikos took her silence as a victory.

'Yes, Nikos.' Kate looked down. 'We are done talking.'

'*Kalos*. Good. If it's any consolation I will endeavour to make your ordeal as short as possible. Rest assured I will do everything within my power to secure Sofia's guardianship as quickly as I can.'

'Thank you.' Kate swallowed hard. 'I know you will.'

'And just so you know...' Nikos moved closer, so she had no alternative but to meet his glittering gaze. 'As of now our honeymoon is officially terminated. For the time being, at least, you are free to return to New York and carry on your life with no interference from me. I will be in contact again when I hear from the courts.'

'Thank you,' Kate repeated quietly. But never had an expression of gratitude rung so hollow or felt so desperately painful to deliver.

CHAPTER TWELVE

CLICKING ON THE SPREADSHEET, Kate stared at the sales figures in amazement. They had shot up, reaching levels way beyond anything she would have conjured up in her wildest dreams only a few weeks ago. With the company's creditors paid off and the order books full again, Kandy Kate had swung into full production once more—the only problem now being how they would meet the demand.

Kate's meeting with Charles Lewis, the CEO of Rosebury's, had been a success. Although, still reeling from her fight with Nikos, she wasn't sure how she had even got through the meeting, let alone managed to secure a deal. But it seemed that American candy was in vogue in Europe at the moment, and in Britain in particular. Rosebury's wanted to market the Kandy Kate brand as an offshoot of their own hugely successful confectionary company. Charles Lewis liked the retro feel, apparently. And he liked her.

He'd been prepared to shake on it there and then, and once news of the deal had hit the stock market, Kandy Kate had been back—big-time. Suddenly everyone was talking about it.

But Kate could take no pleasure from it, felt no pride in her sense of achievement. Instead there was just an empty longing for what could never be. *For Nikos.* Seeing him again, being with him, had confirmed her worst fears. He had stolen a part of her that could never be replaced. She would never be whole without him.

The phone beside her rang and Kate stretched out a hand to reach it. 'Kate O'Connor.'

'Hi, darling, it's your mother.'

Fiona O'Connor hardly needed to explain who she was, her drawl was instantly recognisable.

'Hi, Mom. How are you?' With Kate's mother, this was always a loaded question.

'I'm very well, darling. I've just had another cognitive behavioural therapy session and, do you know, I really believe I am beginning to feel the benefit?'

'That's great, Mom, I'm so pleased.'

'We're working on letting go of the past and focussing on my current issues.'

'Okay…' That sounded like something Kate herself should be doing.

'Tom—that's my personal CB therapist—is the sweetest guy. Nothing is too much trouble for him.'

'So you've settled in well at the clinic? You're happy there?'

Fiona had recently started a twelve-week residential programme at a well-known healing centre in California.

'Darling, it's wonderful—like the most exclusive hotel. The facilities are first-class and the food is out of this world.'

'I'm glad, Mom.' Kate smiled, feeling a little of the weight of responsibility lift from her shoulders. Her mother did seem much happier.

'Goodness knows what it must be costing, though.'

'I've told you—you don't need to worry about that.'

'I know, darling. And I am so thrilled you're making such a success of Kandy Kate now. Your daddy would have been very proud of you.'

Kate swallowed down the familiar lump in her throat that appeared whenever she thought of her father.

'And how's Nikos?' Kate heard Fiona lean into the phone, her voice suddenly conspiratorial.

Kate hesitated. 'He's fine. As far as I know.'

'I'm so pleased everything worked out between you two. I only wish I could have been there for your wedding.'

'Yes, Mom, you already said.' Fiona had done a complete turnaround regarding Nikos's suitability for marrying her daughter, which had been directly and shamelessly directed by the changes in fortune of the two of them. 'Like I told you before, it was just us and a couple of witnesses.'

'I know… I know.' Fiona sighed theatrically. 'But promise me you'll arrange a meeting for the three of us soon—when I'm back in New York. I want to congratulate Nikos in person…welcome him to the family.'

Kate made a non-committal noise. She and Nikos would most likely have gone their separate ways by then, and even if they hadn't it was highly unlikely that Nikos would want to see her mother. Fiona had treated Nikos appallingly when they had first met. Something that still made Kate cringe with embarrassment whenever she thought about it.

'Where is Nikos now?'

Clearly picking up on Kate's hesitation, Fiona honed in on it.

'He's in Athens.'

'Oh, darling, that's no way to start a marriage.' Her mother's voice turned all wistful and concerned. 'You two should be together, making the most of this precious time.'

'It's called *work*, Mom.' Kate clenched her teeth. 'Something we all have to do to pay the bills.'

'Yes, of course, darling. I know. I can be terribly selfish. I hope I'm not too much of a burden to you?'

'You're not a burden, Mom.' Kate drew in a breath. You're my mother and I love you. Getting you well is all that matters.'

'Thank you, darling.' There was a rustle on the line. 'Why, look at the time! I'm going to be late for my massage. Speak soon, darling. Bye!'

'Bye, Mom.'

Kate turned back to her computer. The business was doing well. Her mother seemed much improved. These were two big positives, directly related to her temporary marriage to Nikos.

She had done the right thing even if it didn't feel like it.

It was over a month since she had last seen Nikos. A month that had seen a wall of silence, with no communication from him at all. But still Kate's every thought was full of him. Still she woke every morning with his name on her lips, her heart racing from wild dreams of passion and panic and loss.

Still it felt as if she had an ice pick embedded in her heart.

Nikos curled his toes over the edge of the rock and after taking in a breath performed a perfect swallow dive, hitting the surface with smooth precision. The water felt like silk against his tense muscles and he started a fast crawl out to sea, where the horizon was beginning to turn to liquid gold.

Further and further out he swam, concentrating on the power of his strokes, the next intake of breath, the sense of being at one with the sea. It felt good, blotting everything out like this, focussing solely on putting as much distance between himself and the shore as he could, leaving his life behind him.

But the relief was only temporary. With his muscles starting to complain, his chest burning, Nikos finally slowed his pace and turned onto his back, surprised to see how far he had swum. Reluctantly he started to head back. Because there was no escape from his life.

These past few weeks he had tried—God knew he had tried—but nothing had worked. Nothing could rid him of the presence of Kate in his head—the torment, the temptation, the wild intensity of feelings that grabbed him by the throat and shook him till he rattled.

After leaving London he had flown to Athens, where his company headquarters were based. Seeking refuge in work again, he had driven himself harder, pushed himself further, intent on finding some sort of normality in the cut and thrust of a business deal or the quiet security of figures and spreadsheets.

But there was no normality to be had. No matter how much he tried to distract himself, everything came back to Kate.

His reaction to that photograph in the newspaper had been extreme. The shock of seeing her like that had overridden every rational thought. Caught up in his initial fury, he had assumed that Kate had to be guilty in some way, that she must have come on to this guy, or allowed him to come on to her, and things had got out of hand. His every instinct had been screaming at him that Kate couldn't be trusted, that she was a liability, a ticking time bomb.

But as the days had passed reason had crept in. She would hardly have been initiating sex with a stranger in a pub's beer garden with a crowd of people around her, including Sofia. Maybe he shouldn't have reacted so violently. Maybe he should have listened to her explanation.

But the fact was it had happened, and it had been plastered all over the press. And if the Greek courts chose to believe it, it would pose a real threat to his becoming Sofia's guardian. That in itself was enough to settle a red mist over him.

He had contacted the courts straight away—ostensibly to enquire as to how the case was proceeding, but really to put out feelers to see if he could sense any change of mood. He hadn't detected anything untoward, but even so he'd followed it up with more communication, stressing the need to have the court hearing as soon as possible, trying to speed the process up.

He wasn't sure how far he was getting with

that, but at least he wasn't sensing any new issues holding it up. Maybe they had got away with it.

That was one small comfort. But it wasn't enough. It couldn't douse the fire in his belly that still raged for Kate—for who she was, for what she had done to him, for everything she meant to him.

With his turmoil impacting on the way he worked, the treatment of his staff, it had finally fallen to his PA to tell him to stop behaving like such a jerk. Not that she had phrased it quite like that, but he had got the message.

Lovely Madeline…who had worked with him ever since he had opened his office…who brought in homemade pastries…who came in early, stayed late…for whom nothing was too much trouble. Madeline who had proudly presented him with a wedding gift on the first day of his return to the office—an elaborately wrapped affair that he still hadn't had the heart to open, accompanied by a huge card signed by all his Athens staff.

Clearly she had drawn the short straw, as she had nervously approached him one day and suggested that he needed a break from work. That maybe he should return to Crete for a while. She had told him that she would take care of things at the office. Anyone else and he would have bitten their heads off, fired them on the spot for their impudence. But looking into Madeline's soft, wise eyes he had found himself agreeing. Thinking maybe she was right.

She had put his private jet on standby before he'd even got back to his desk.

Back on the shore, Nikos roughly towelled himself down and pulled on his shorts.

Stepping away from Kate, putting some space between them, had been the right decision. There was nothing to be gained by torment-ing each other still further. Certainly nothing to be gained by raking over the past. As far as he was concerned that fateful night was dead and buried—along with the man he had been then. The resentment he felt for Kate and her mother was still there, but picking over the bones would achieve nothing.

But Kate had insisted on dragging it all out, making him say things he hadn't wanted to say, opening up about his background when he'd had no intention of doing any such thing. She'd even tried to make out that she had found his impov-erished state attractive, when they both knew that was a damned lie. She had tried to get him to show her his hurt when all he'd wanted to do was show her his strength.

The longer he'd spent in Kate's company, the more he'd known he was in danger of being sucked under. He had felt himself weakening, his hard-won resolve slipping through his fingers minute by minute, second by second. With his resistance being steadily chipped away, he had been in danger of becoming completely obsessed with Kate. *Again.* And look how that had turned out last time.

So he'd had to be strong. To assert his authority and assume command. It was essential that Kate knew who called the shots, who held all the power. Because that was *him*. He had engineered her back into his life. He had known exactly what he was doing when he had taken her to his bed. *He* was in control.

Which meant he had to stop his brain from craving more. From making the hideous mistake of thinking that he needed Kate in his life, not just his bed. Of thinking that he wanted to make her his—permanently.

Flinging his towel over his shoulder, he was about to head back to the villa when the fiery sunset blazing across the sky stopped him in his tracks. He stood with his hands on his hips to watch the spectacle. Crete was full of beautiful beaches, but somehow he had been inexorably drawn to this one. To the beach where he had proposed to Kate…to the exact spot where the deed had been done. It was as if he was deliberately torturing himself.

It seemed there was no escaping the memories of her.

CHAPTER THIRTEEN

THE AEROPLANE BANKED steeply before starting its descent, giving Kate a slanting picture of the island of Crete below, bathed in early-evening sunshine, the turquoise water fringing white sandy coves, the dense greenery and the craggy mountains further inland. Just beautiful.

She remembered her first sighting of this view. Just starting her European adventure, she had fallen in love with the place before the plane had even landed—had felt excitement bubbling inside her at the thought of being able to spend time somewhere so idyllic. Back then she'd had no idea of what ecstasy and misery the island had in store for her. No premonition that the next few weeks would change her life for ever.

'If you would like to put on your seat belt, Kyria Nikoladis, we will be landing in ten minutes.'

Kate smiled her thanks at the flight attendant and fastened the buckle around her waist. Her every need had been catered for on this transatlantic flight. Even though Kate had made it clear she could easily take a scheduled flight, Nikos had insisted that she made use of his private jet. No doubt he wanted her back in Crete as fast as possible, with no excuse for any delay.

The phone call had come early yesterday morning.

Kate had imagined Nikos's impatience, waiting for New York to wake up a full seven hours behind Crete. She'd heard it in his voice when she'd answered, still half asleep, and had felt shock and surprise shooting through her, followed by a wave of anxiety. And all before she had even said hello. It was the first time she had heard from him in weeks.

Nikos needed her back in Crete, apparently. Right away. This he had informed her in a coldly determined way, clearly designed to brook no argument. If he had been expecting her to refuse, to kick off and say she would do no such thing, he needn't have worried. Kate would honour the agreement between them. Nikos had fulfilled his side of the bargain and she would do the same. That, at least, was clear-cut. Even if everything else between them was a murky pool of misery and regret.

Crossing the concourse towards a waiting limousine, Kate shielded her eyes against the glare of the setting sun. The driver opened the door for her and, taking a deep breath, Kate slid inside.

Disappointment hit her like a sledgehammer. He wasn't there. Just an empty space where she had hoped Nikos would be. She quickly pulled herself together. Why would he come to meet her? It was hardly as if he was dying to see her.

The journey to Villa Levanda, Nikos's luxurious home, took no more than twenty minutes. Kate had never been there before. When she had met first Nikos he had been living in a little stone cottage belonging to his cousin. Kate had loved it. She had loved *him*. Now that humble residence had been swapped for a huge gleaming glass construction perched on the edge of a cliff.

So much had changed. Those reckless young lovers were gone—replaced by level-headed adults making sensible decisions to further their own ends. *In theory, at least.* Deep down Kate knew she still felt the same. She still loved Nikos with all her heart. And that realisation made each heavy beat more painful than the last.

There was no sign of Nikos when the driver let her in, depositing her small case on the floor beside her and leaving her in the care of the housekeeper, who introduced herself as Agní.

Showing her to her room, Agní fussed about, making sure everything was to her satisfaction, until Kate assured her that it was and that she was going to go straight to bed, because she was exhausted from the travelling. After a quick shower in the gleaming glass bathroom Kate pulled back the white covers on the enormous bed and slid underneath, hoping for the oblivion of sleep.

A tap on the door interrupted her. Suddenly the room was filled with the darkly powerful presence of Nikos, sucking the oxygen out of the air, making Kate's heart pound.

She scrambled out of bed, instinctively starting to cross the room towards him, then stopped abruptly, asking herself what on earth she thought she was doing, rushing at him as if he would be pleased to see her—as if he was going to gather her in his arms, hold her close, whisper a greeting seductively in her ear. *If only.*

She took a couple of steps backwards.

'Hi.'

'*Yassou.*'

His eyes moved over her like the touch of his hands, taking in the skimpy satin slip nightie, the swell of her breasts, her bare legs, the way her chest rose and fell with a sudden shortness of breath.

'I'm sorry—I have disturbed you?'

'No.' *Not unless you count the way every nerve in my body has pulled taut, or how my heart is slamming in my chest.* 'I wasn't asleep.'

'I just wanted to make sure you have everything you need.'

'Yes.' Kate gazed back at him. 'Agní was very attentive.'

'I was taking a conference call when you arrived, otherwise I would have come to meet you myself.'

'It's fine, Nikos. You don't need to explain.' Kate was drinking in the sight of him. The hard perfection of him and the fluid grace as he came towards her was holding her captive, turning her bones to rubber.

'Thank you for coming.'

He was right in front of her now, his expression strangely uncertain. Close up, Kate could see the tension in his muscles, could sense beneath the savage beauty an edgy energy that he seemed to be struggling to contain. She felt the knot inside her tighten. She longed to reach out to him, to run her fingertips along the shadow of stubble covering his jaw, to raise them to his mouth, to part his lips and wait for him to suck her fingers, the way he had the very first time they had made love.

She drank in his dark beauty. A black sleeveless vest emphasised the hard perfection of his biceps and faded khaki shorts revealed long, bronzed legs. His hair had grown, and was now curling at the nape of his neck, tousled, as if he had been worrying at it with an impatient hand.

Kate realised he looked more like the old Nikos than at any time since he had first walked back into her life. More Greek, more Cretan—as if he had come home. Which, of course, he had. She blinked down the lump in her throat.

'After the way we parted I wasn't sure you would come.' His soft statement broke the silence.

'After the way we parted I wasn't sure you would want me.' Her reply revealed more than she had meant it to. Even though that photograph in the paper hadn't been her fault, she had still worried herself senseless over the past few weeks that it might have ruined Nikos's chances of becoming Sofia's guardian. 'Do you know how the court case is progressing?'

'My lawyers seem confident.'

She waited for him to elaborate, but it seemed Nikos intended to say no more on the subject. Kate let out a pent-up breath. She would take that for now. 'Well, that's good.'

'Yes.'

Nikos inched a step further towards her, his dark eyes boring into her, raising her core temperature by several degrees.

'Congratulations on securing the deal with Rosebury's, by the way. I heard Charles Lewis was very impressed by you.'

'Thanks.' Kate swallowed hard. He was so close now she that was enveloped in Nikos's warm, male scent, all her senses caught in his spell. 'I think it will prove to be very profitable for Kandy Kate.'

'I'm sure…'

He lowered his head so that his breath whispered across her upturned face. He radiated a hot sexual energy that sent her core throbbing with need. But still he didn't touch her. Outwardly they were being so formal, so polite, but inside Kate was dying with longing. And, judging by the way he was gazing at her, his pupils dilated, his features harsh with lust, Nikos was feeling it too.

'The court hearing is at ten a.m. tomorrow.' He continued to talk practicalities. 'I have arranged for us to meet with the lawyers an hour beforehand to go over a few things.'

'Sure.'

'Thanks for doing this, Kate.'

He'd lowered his voice. The air thrummed with silent awareness at the slight shift in tone. As if she were standing on the edge of a cliff, Kate knew that one false move would be all that it took to see her fall.

'We have a deal.' She fought to hold her voice steady, hold *herself* steady. 'I would never renege on that.'

'No, of course not.'

Still he didn't move. The world held its breath.

'Well, if you're sure there's nothing you need I will say goodnight.'

Kate gave a small nod. Her heart thundered in her chest. It would be the easiest thing in the world to reach out to him now, thread her fingers through his hair, pull his lips down to hers and start to kiss him. To fan the smouldering embers of their desire and let it burst into flames.

Kate trembled at the thought of it. She wanted it so badly she ached for it. Burned for it. Her whole being was consumed with hunger for him.

'*Kalinikta*, Kate.'

'Goodnight, Nikos.' *I love you.*

The words appeared from nowhere, ringing loudly in her head. But no way would she speak them out loud.

Pressing the heels of her palms against her closed eyelids, she watched flashes of amber light cutting through the darkness.

When she took her hands away, he was gone.

'We did it!'

Stepping out into the bright sunshine, Nikos pulled Kate into a fierce hug. He let himself hold her for a moment, breathing her in, relishing the soft contours of her body pressed against his. He had spent so long forbidding himself from touching her that he was going to revel in this moment of triumph.

When he'd seen her standing there in her bedroom last night, looking so unbelievably sexy in that slip of a nightie, it had taken every scrap of willpower he possessed to stop himself from kissing her. He'd wanted her so badly he had been physically shaking with the power of it.

He should never have gone in there, of course. His flimsy excuse that he needed to tell her about the time of the court hearing had been about as fake as his declaration to himself that she meant nothing to him.

Now, with her pressed against his chest, he knew he wanted her more than anything he had ever wanted in his entire life. He knew she meant everything to him. And his stocks of willpower were all used up.

'Congratulations!' Kate pulled back to look at him, her eyes shining brightly. 'I can't tell you how pleased I am!'

'*Evcharisto*, Kate.' He stared at her, giddy with relief. 'Thank you so much for your support.'

'You are more than welcome.' Kate smiled into his eyes.

In the end the court hearing had been short and very sweet. With the weight of Nikos's legal team making itself felt, and supported by a letter from Sofia stating how much she wanted Nikos to be her guardian, the only other contender—

Sofia's great-uncle—had decided to withdraw his claim.

The courts, having looked into Nikos's background and found him to be a man of good character, had ascertained that he was in a stable marriage, to a woman Sofia liked, and had decided that he was capable of accepting the full responsibility of guardianship, and permission had been granted there and then. And a burden that Nikos hadn't fully realised he had been carrying around with him had immediately been lifted from his shoulders.

His lawyers came out onto the steps behind them, and with many handshakes and some back-slapping, Nikos thanked them too. This was a good day.

'We must let Sofia know.' Kate clutched at his sleeve.

Nikos pulled out his phone and within seconds Sofia was screaming her delight. Laughing, Nikos put her on speakerphone, looking at Kate as Sofia switched to English, babbling with happiness.

'You must go out and celebrate!'

'And we will—as soon as you are back in Crete,' Nikos said.

'No, I mean you two—right away!' Sofia's reply was vehement. 'I've got exams, so I won't be back for weeks. But I insist that you both go and get totally drunk in honour of the occasion.'

'Hmm... Not sure what the courts would make of *that*.'

'It's too late—they can't do anything now. You're stuck with me.'

'And very happy I am to be stuck too.' Nikos smiled into the phone.

'So go on—what are you waiting for? Off you go. Get a bottle of champagne opened!'

'We can't celebrate properly without you,' Kate interjected quickly.

There was a pause before Sofia replied in a *very* knowing tone. 'Oh, yes, I think you can...'

Standing nervously on the edge of the cliff, Kate looked down. A long, *long* way down. Sea birds swooped below her and sunlight sparkled on the vast expanse of blue water. She took in a deep breath of the tangy salty air. There was a stiff breeze up here, ruffling her hair, flapping her cream silk blouse against her chest. It was ex-hilarating, intoxicating... It made her feel alive.

When Nikos had suggested they should have a

picnic lunch to celebrate Kate had immediately agreed. With a stab to her heart, she had known it might potentially be the last time she ever saw him. Now the court case was over she served no useful purpose in his life.

Tomorrow she was flying to London for a meeting with Rosebury's, then back to New York. The thought of leaving Nikos, being parted from him for ever, filled her with a dread so heavy that it was simply too horrendous to contemplate. So Kate was going to live for the moment. If this was their last chance to spend some time together, she was going to grab it. Maybe the scars of their past were too deep, too painful ever to be overcome. But on a beautiful day like this, with the sun high in the sky and Nikos's mood equally soaring, there was no way she was going to turn him down.

Although his choice of venue wasn't for the faint-hearted...

Driving on the twisty coast road back towards the villa, which boasted a series of hairpin bends that had her hanging onto the edge of her seat, Nikos had suddenly pulled the car off the road in a spray of dust and told her that they were here. He had arranged for a picnic to be delivered to a cove at the foot of these cliffs. They just had to climb down to get there.

Neither of them was exactly dressed for rock-climbing—Nikos wearing tailored suit trousers and Kate equally formal in a smart navy skirt. But now, as Nikos stretched out his hand, promising to see her safely down to the bottom, Kate took it confidently, knowing he would do just that. Her faith in him was absolute.

Suddenly she realised he was the one man in the world she would trust with her life. But trusting him with her love…? That was a very different prospect.

Following a steep, overgrown pathway strewn with boulders, they picked their way down, Nikos a couple of steps ahead, frequently turning to stop and help Kate, his grip strong and warm as he took her hand or her arm, his eyes twinkling mischievously as he smiled at her. With the wind tossing his dark curls, Kate didn't think she had ever seen him look more devastatingly handsome.

Near the bottom of the cliffs the rocks were wet and slippery, where a mountain stream trickled over them, so Nikos instructed her to put her arms around his neck. Sliding one hand under her thighs, he used the other to steady himself against the cliff-face. Pressed against his hot, muscled torso, her face buried into his neck, Kate breathed in his manly scent, her eyes closing with dizzy pleasure. She wished she could bottle this moment to keep for ever.

Their destination was a perfect little cove of fine white sand, encircled by cliffs that made it completely private. Miraculously, the picnic was already there, waiting for them. A white awning had been erected to give them some shade, with cotton rugs spread underneath and a neat row of cool boxes lined up in readiness.

Laughing at Kate's naïve question about how his staff had managed to get all this stuff down the cliff, Nikos explained that it had come by boat. Shielding his eyes against the sun, he pointed out the direction of his villa and the launch boat, quietly anchored a few metres from the shore, that had been left for their return. He had clearly thought of everything.

Even, Kate discovered, a neatly packed bag especially for her, containing sunscreen, a wide-brimmed straw hat and a pretty white bikini that fitted perfectly when Kate nervously slipped it on. When she expressed her surprise, Nikos matter-of-factly informed her that Agní had chosen it.

With the contents of the cool boxes spread out on the rugs before them, they ate lunch at a leisurely pace, sharing morsels of the delicious food between them, savouring it with quiet groans of appreciation.

Refilling their glasses with chilled champagne, Nikos handed Kate's to her. *'Yamas.'*

'Cheers.'

Raising herself onto one elbow, Kate accepted it with a smile. She would definitely have to make this one her last, though. Already the combination of sun, sea and champagne had gone to her head. And that was before she factored in the lethal presence of Nikos, who lounged beside her in a pair of brief trunks, his olive-skinned, super-toned body on full display.

'I might go for a swim.' Setting down his glass, Nikos rose to his feet, his figure so tall that it blocked out the sun.

Kate gazed up at him. Bronzed and muscled, he looked like some sort of Greek god. A perfect specimen of manhood in every respect—as his brief black trunks attested.

'Will you join me?'

'No.' Kate tore her eyes away. 'I'm going to wait a little after all that wonderful food. You go, though.'

Nikos nodded, and as he turned to stride towards the sea Kate allowed her eyes to feast upon him again, taking in the play of muscles across his shoulders, the narrow waist, the gorgeous tight butt. She hugged her knees tight, trying hard to stem the tide of longing inside her. But it was hopeless. She loved Nikos with all her heart and with every fibre of her being. And it would always be that way.

She watched as he waded powerfully into the water, then dived under the surface, reappearing further out. With a sigh Kate lay back, putting her straw hat over her face and staring up at the pinpricks of light. Within minutes she was asleep.

Nikos walked back up the beach towards where Kate lay so peacefully on the rug. When she didn't stir at his approach he realised she was asleep under her sun hat, and quietly he settled himself down beside her.

His eyes travelled the length of her body from the painted toenails on her pretty feet to her long legs, one bent so that it rested against the other, and on to the hollow of her tummy, her ribcage rising and falling with each soft breath, and the swell of her small breasts beneath the flimsy bikini top.

Nikos swallowed hard. His craving for Kate had reached dangerous proportions, slamming into him with hot hard waves, each one more powerful than the last. So all-consuming it made it difficult to breathe, rang in his ears like a warning, blurred his vision. A long, cool dip in the sea had done nothing to cool his fervour—as the painful swell in his trunks made all too clear.

He leant over her, watching the way his shadow fell across her torso. His physical reaction to her needed no explanation—it was obvious: she was completely gorgeous. Far more complex were the other emotions she stirred in him. Affection, tenderness, and the primal urge to protect her from harm, to keep her safe.

She gave him comfort too. Waiting for the court to announce its decision that morning, he had realised that having Kate by his side *mattered*. Not because they were keeping up appearances, but because she made him strong, made him feel better—about the court case, Sofia,

Philippos, about life in general. When she had lightly laid her hand on top of his, giving it an encouraging squeeze, he had been deeply touched. Far more than the modest act had warranted. Far more than he wanted to examine.

But recently he had been forced to examine a lot of things about Kate that he would have preferred to ignore. Her empathy, for example, and the respectful way she treated everyone from the staff at the hotels they'd stayed in to the self-important businessmen they'd dined with. Then there was her kindness towards Sofia—how she had gone out of her way to try and make her birthday special, even if that particular venture had backfired. And her loyalty...

Nikos could see now that Kate's loyalty to her family was at the heart of everything she did. By saving Kandy Kate she was resurrecting her father's name, preserving it for posterity. He could even see now why she had sided with her mother when he had turned up in New York. Fiona O'Connor obviously had problems that ran more deeply than he'd realised. And today he'd had a little bit of that loyalty directed at him and it had warmed his soul. Not only that, but it had left him wanting more.

Unable to stand the temptation a minute longer, Nikos dipped his head, planting the lightest of kisses on Kate's tummy button. Kate stirred, very slightly, and then went still again. Using the tip of his tongue, he circled her navel, then trailed his tongue upwards, its touch featherlight. She smelled of suntan lotion and she tasted of sunshine.

With his heart thundering in his chest, Nikos edged closer. Her face was hidden beneath the hat, so he couldn't see her expression, but he knew she was awake now—he could tell by the quickening of her breath, the way her hands lying at her sides had begun to twitch.

His trembling fingers found the ties at the side of her bikini top and pulled the knots free. He lifted the triangles of fabric to expose her breasts. Ruby nipples peaked hard and he took one in his hot, wet mouth, closing his eyes as sucked strongly, encouraged by a moan of pleasure from Kate. By the time he had turned his attention to the second breast Kate was squirming, arching her back, her hands clawing into the mat beneath her.

So nearly there. There was only one thing Nikos wanted more than to plunge the hard length of himself into the silky wet softness of Kate, and that was for her to command him to do it. He needed to see her face, to see what was going on behind those beautiful deep green eyes.

Reaching forward, Nikos lifted the hat from her face and tossed it to one side. Kate's eyes were tightly shut, her cheeks flushed, her mouth open.

'Look at me, Kate.' His command held all the urgency of a man very, *very* close to the point of losing his self-control.

Kate did as she was told, her thick, dark lashes lifting tantalisingly slowly, revealing emerald eyes that glittered like the most precious jewels. Nikos stared into them, drinking in their beauty, their infinite depth, registering everything they were telling him.

And that was all he needed. As the tip of her tongue reached out to wet the velvet plumpness of her lips he gave himself permission to let go, bending his head to place his mouth over hers, immediately lost in the power of their kiss.

Turning onto her side, Kate looped her leg over his hip, pressing their bodies together, hot skin against hot skin. Sliding his hand between them, Nikos slipped his hand beneath her bikini bottoms, his fingers finding her soft, sweet core. With a sharp spasm and a gasp of pleasure into his mouth Kate let her tongue tangle with his, hot and wet and wild.

Without breaking the kiss Nikos rolled onto his back, so that Kate was above him, and then, lifting her hips, firmly positioned her over his throbbing groin.

There was no going back now.

CHAPTER FOURTEEN

IT WAS EVENING by the time they returned to
Villa Levanda, Nikos having skilfully manoeuvred the launch boat into the small mooring at
the foot of the cliff, leapt ashore to secure the
ropes, then held out a hand to assist Kate. Silence settled over them as they climbed the steep
steps leading to the villa, and Kate hung on to
the wooden handrail warmed by the sun to help
her to the top.

She was exhausted. Mentally and physically
spent. Today had been so wonderful, so perfect
in every way, but now, as the villa came into
view, she knew the day was nearly at an end. Everything was nearly at an end, and the cold fingers of reality started to close around her heart.

Ahead of her, Nikos was juggling cool boxes
and bags of beach equipment, but at the top he
stopped and put them down, turning to look at
Kate. 'You okay?'

'Sure.'

It was an automatic response—a word she had probably used tens of thousands of times—but never had it felt less true. Because Kate *wasn't* okay. Far from it.

As she joined Nikos at the top and looked back at the panoramic view, darkening around her, she felt emptied out…barren. Like an echoing space that could only ever be filled by one man. Nikos.

'Come on, you look done in.' Leaving the bags, Nikos slipped his hand around her waist and guided her towards the villa. 'You need a shower and a meal and an early night. We both do.'

He turned and gave her a mischievous smile that crinkled the corners of his eyes, lighting up his handsome face. Kate thought she was going to cry.

The villa was cool and quiet, and Kate quickly made her way to her room, leaving Nikos no time to say he would join her. Standing under the shower, she let the pounding water cascade over her, watching the rivulets of soap run over her lightly tanned body, the fine grains of sand accumulating at her feet.

Refusing to look at her face in the mirror, afraid of what she might see, Kate towelled herself dry, then pulled on a white kaftan and slipped her feet into a pair of sandals. She had decided she was going to tell Nikos that she didn't want anything to eat. That she needed an early night. Alone. It was time to put an end to this agonising torture.

But, walking into the living room, she found it empty. Hearing the clink of cutlery coming from the terrace, she wandered out and saw Agní laying the table there.

'*Kalispera, kyria.*' She straightened up, smoothing down her apron. 'I hope you have had a pleasant day?'

'Yes, thank you.' Kate felt a blush creep over her cheeks. Surely it must be obvious what she and Nikos had been doing? Kate felt as if she was still radiating sexual energy. 'And, please, call me Kate.'

'Of course… Kate.' Agní smiled slightly nervously. 'I am so pleased to hear the news about Sofia.'

'Isn't it great?' Kate agreed wholeheartedly. Then a thought occurred to her. 'Do you know Sofia, then?'

'Yes. She is the same age as my younger sister. They were in the same class before… Well, before Sofia was sent to boarding school. My sister was there to support her at Philippos's funeral, though. We all were.'

'Well, I'm sure she appreciated that.'

'And now she will be living here at Villa Levanda, at least for the holidays, so we will be able to see much more of her.' Agní smiled happily.

'Yes, of course.'

Kate looked away, fighting back tears. She knew it was horribly selfish of her, but she couldn't match Agní's cheerfulness. She was talking about a shared history that Kate knew nothing about. And worse—far worse—about a shared future that she would never be part of.

'*Efharisto*, Agní.'

Nikos appeared, smelling of citrus soap, his damp hair curling at the nape of his neck. He was wearing a plain white tee shirt and loose navy cotton trousers. Kate drank in the sight of him. After a rapid conversation with Agní in Greek, he pulled out a chair for Kate, who was still standing awkwardly beside the table.

'Agní has made her special moussaka for us. I guarantee it will be the best moussaka you have ever tasted.'

'Great…' Kate tried to smile. She could hardly refuse to eat the meal now—it would appear rude.

Nikos reached for the wine bottle in the cooler, but when he went to fill Kate's glass Kate shook her head. If she was to share this last meal with Nikos, she didn't want it to be blurred by alcohol. Suddenly she knew she wanted to live every last second with him. She wanted to feel the pleasure and the pain. Because no one else would be able to make her experience emotions like this again.

Nikos swapped the wine for sparkling water, filling his own glass too, before taking Kate's hand, which lay on the table between them. He turned the plain gold wedding ring on her finger, staring at it intently.

As if returning from a trance, he replaced her hand on the table and met her eyes. 'So, what time is your meeting with Rosebury's tomorrow?'

'Um…three-thirty.' Kate had arranged to meet with Charles Lewis to go over the forecasts for Kandy Kate in the UK. 'There's a nine a.m. flight that should get me there in plenty of time.'

'You don't want to take the private jet? It's yours if you want it.'

'No, thank you.' Kate took a sip of water. 'I'm

very grateful for all your help—with Kandy Kate and everything else—but now I need to stand on my own two feet.'

'If you're sure?'

'I am.'

Silence fell between them, punctuated only by the cicadas in the olive trees and the rustle of the sea breeze.

'Then I guess this is it.'

Kate bit down on her lip. She would not cry. *She would not cry.*

'At some point we will have to see about a divorce.' As he spoke the night air stilled. 'But I don't suppose there's any hurry.'

'Not unless you want to remarry!' Kate had rushed to try and fill the aching gap. But her attempt at levity only worsened the pain.

Nikos made a disbelieving noise in his throat. 'Or you, of course.'

'Yes.' Kate's fingernails bit into her palms. 'Or me.'

Agní appeared, proudly bearing a large dish of steaming moussaka, and set it on the table before them before discreetly disappearing.

Nikos quickly served them, then raised his

glass of water. 'A toast, then.' His eyes shone almost black. 'To the future.'

'Yes.' Kate touched her glass against his. 'The future.'

'I wish you every happiness Kate. You do know that, don't you? I really hope you find what you're looking for.'

What she was looking for? Kate's bottom lip began to tremble. Could Nikos really not see that what she was looking for—everything she could ever want—was right in front of her? Did he really not *know*? Or was he making it plain that it could never be? Twisting the knife with his gentle words and telling her that they were done—finished? *That he could never love her.*

She took another gulp of water. 'You too, Nikos.' Somehow she formed the words from her strangled throat.

For a long moment Nikos held her gaze. Unable to look away, Kate lost herself in the fathomless depths of his eyes, falling down and down to a place from which she could never return. She didn't even want to.

'Kate?'

Eventually he spoke. Never had her name on his lips sounded more solemn, more portentous.

'Yes?' The word quaked with a mixture of fear and hope.

But silence fell between them again, as if time was holding its breath.

'Nothing.' He turned his proud profile away, staring out to sea. 'It doesn't matter.'

'No, go on.' She reached across the table for his hand. 'What were you going to say?'

'No, really…it was nothing.' The moment had gone, like a glimmer of sunshine engulfed by clouds. 'Come on—eat up. You've hardly touched your food.'

'I'm afraid I don't have much appetite.' Kate withdrew her hand.

'No.' Nikos moved his plate away. 'Me neither. Not for food, anyway.'

With a sudden movement he pushed back his chair and stood up. Startled, Kate felt her heart plummet to her feet.

Was this goodbye? Oh, please no.

Silently Nikos walked round to the back of her chair, lightly placing his hands on her shoulders. Kate closed her eyes.

'One last night?'

His question whispered around her like a heady, seductive promise. Relief swamped her.

Not trusting herself to speak, she turned to look up at him, swallowing hard. She felt herself nod. A small, almost imperceptible movement. But it was all that was needed.

Pulling back her chair, Nikos waited for her to stand then, taking her hand, he led her into his bedroom, closing the door firmly behind them.

Nikos rolled on his side, stretching out an arm to where Kate should be. Nothing. He opened his eyes.

She had gone.

Leaping out of bed, he threw open the bedroom door, marching through the living room to Kate's bedroom, already knowing it would be empty. And so it was. There was no evidence of Kate having stayed the night there at all. Not so much as an open drawer or a slight indentation on the neatly made bed.

Cursing, Nikos stormed back to his own room, hurrying to cover his nakedness with some hastily thrown on clothes. Lifting his head, he found himself staring straight into Kate's eyes. Her portrait, drawn by the artist in Paris, gazed back at him, taunting him with a watchful gaze. Having it framed and hung in his bedroom had felt like a guilty secret. Now it seemed more like masochism.

How could she have left without him knowing? He had been awake most of the night—at first totally consumed by the after-effects of their lovemaking and then, when Kate had finally fallen asleep, staring at her head on the pillow, at the dark sweep of her lashes, the soft fullness of her lips, listening to her gentle breathing, inhaling her intoxicating scent.

Under the cover of darkness he had allowed himself that one sweet indulgence. He wasn't going to try and rationalise his feelings, to attempt to make sense of anything.

What was there to rationalise anyway? *He loved her.* It was a certain, indisputable fact.

And maybe that was the very definition of love—it wasn't rational. It was the most exquisite, excruciating, punishingly powerful feeling in the world. And every breath he took hurt with it. But what was he to do?

In the end, Kate had made the decision for him.

As dawn had started to creep across the sky, when Nikos had finally fallen asleep, she had pulled back the covers, left the sanctuary of their bed and walked out of his life for ever.

No! Not if Nikos had any say in it! If he dashed to the airport he might be in time to stop her. And if he wasn't he would fly to London himself. In his private jet he would probably get there before her.

Snatching up his passport, he jammed it into his back pocket and headed for the door.

And then he saw it. Kate's wedding ring, lying on the glass table by the front door.

Nikos stopped, his heart pounding in his chest. She must have pulled it off just as she was leaving. He stared hard at the simple gold band, narrowing his eyes as if somehow it held the clue to their future. To everything.

Had Kate thrown it down, relieved that she no longer had to pretend to be shackled to Yhim? Or had she slowly, reluctantly eased it from her finger, experiencing at least some feeling of regret before placing it carefully on the table?

The ring wasn't revealing its secrets, and in the end what did it matter? Their marriage was effectively over. They had both fulfilled their obligations to one another. As he had said to Kate last night—this was it…the end. And she had said nothing to dispute it.

Picking up the ring, Nikos held it between his

thumb and forefinger, turning it to catch the light. He had been so near to asking her to stay. Teetering on the very brink of confessing his need for her, his love for her. Would it have made any difference if he had? Or would he simply have been laying himself open to more ridicule, more heartbreak?

He had been hurt so badly once by Kate, and only a fool would go back for more. But where Kate was concerned he *was* a fool. The biggest fool going. He had given her every opportunity to talk to him, to show him some sort of sign that she wanted to stay. They had shared the most wonderful night together.

And how had Kate rewarded him? By sneaking out of the house while he was still asleep. Without having the decency to even say goodbye.

Palming the ring, he closed his fist over it, watching the skin pull taut over his knuckles. *Enough!* He would not play victim to this woman any more.

Shoving the ring into his pocket without looking at it again, he turned on his heel and marched back through to the living room. Sliding open the enormous glass doors, he walked out onto the terrace, where the reassuring sound of the cicadas, the dazzling light and the sunshine twinkling on the broad expanse of water heralded another new day.

Nikos made himself stop and stare, forcing himself to be grateful for what he had—a wonderful home, a hugely successful business empire. And now he had guardianship of Sofia all his goals had been met. All except one.

There was still one thing he wanted in the world above all else. *Kate.* Without her there was a yawning chasm in his life—so huge, so wide, it could never be crossed. But he would not beg. Kate had made her decision. Despite every instinct screaming at him to go after her, he had to let her go.

Time passed.

Finding it impossible to settle to anything, Nikos paced around the villa, then went into the gardens, taking the steps down to the water's edge and staring out to sea. Usually a source of solace, today it held no comfort for him. Even the thought of going out on his boat did nothing to ease his misery.

How was he going to live the rest of his life without her? It was unthinkable.

A dozen times he picked up his phone to call

her, but a dozen times he put it down. He would not be that weak. He would not be that man. His heart might be breaking, but at least he had his pride. He would not let Kate take that away from him.

Eventually he ended up back on the terrace, gazing unseeing into the distance. Hearing a noise behind him, he stiffened. He had sent Agní home. And nobody ever visited his remote villa uninvited.

'Nikos…'

Her soft voice floated towards him like a promise on the breeze. *Kate*. Nikos gripped the arms of his chair, fighting every instinct to leap up and go to her, to silence the madness in his head by taking her in his arms and never letting go.

With superhuman effort, he remained seated. 'Did you forget something?' He spoke over his shoulder.

'In a way, yes.'

He heard her come closer, moving around the side of the villa.

'Well, go ahead and find it.' He kept his voice firm, harsh, still staring straight ahead. 'Don't let me stop you.'

'I… I already did.'

He heard her falter.

'I came back to find you.'

'Me?' Nikos started to turn, but she was right behind him now.

Kate's hands came down on his shoulders, softly restraining him. 'No, don't turn around, Nikos. Don't look at me. I can't do this if your eyes are on me.'

'Do what?'

He heard her draw in a juddering breath.

'Make my confession.'

Confession? Nikos's thoughts flew wildly in every direction. But when he spoke his words were cold. 'Go on.'

'I love you.'

She loved him.

Her words slowly sank into him, warming him like the golden sun.

She loved him.

He tried to move but Kate's hands pressed down harder.

'No, hear me out, Nikos. If I don't say it now I will lose my nerve.' Her light gasp split the air. 'I have loved you from the very first moment I set eyes on you and that love has only grown deeper and stronger. Even when we were apart—even when you'd hurt me so badly—I still loved you. I have come back to tell you this because suddenly I couldn't bear for you not to know the truth. Not to know the way I feel about you. You are the only man I have ever loved, or ever could love.'

She paused, her breath catching in her throat.

'There—it's done. I've said it.' She gave a short, brave laugh. 'Now you only have to say the word and I will go.'

'Go?' Nikos repeated the word in a daze. A split second later he was on his feet, hurling the metal chair between them to one side with a clatter. 'No, Kate!' He moved his arms around her waist, roughly drawing her to him. 'You mustn't go. Not now—not ever.'

'But...'

'There are no buts, Kate.' He looked deep into her eyes. 'I want you to stay by my side for ever. I want you to be my wife in the real sense of the word...in *every* sense of the word. Because... because...'

'Yes?' Her voice was a small, cracked whisper.

'Because I love you too, Kate.' He lowered his voice. 'More than you will ever know.'

'Oh, Nikos!' Flinging her arms around his neck, Kate raised herself up on tiptoes, moving her hands to cup his face tenderly. 'Are you sure?'

She gazed at him, blinking back the emotion that Nikos could see was so nearly ready to spill over.

'Yes, Kate. More sure than I have ever been about anything in my entire life.' He planted the softest of kisses on her lips. 'Deep down I have known it all along, but I've been so blinded by hurt and pride and downright stubbornness that I've refused to admit it. Even to myself.'

'I guess we're both guilty of those traits.' Kate gave him a rueful smile.

'True. But you weren't to know that beneath my cocky exterior lay a man riddled with insecurities.'

Nikos saw the flicker of confusion on Kate's face as his admission sank in.

'Really?' She stared at him in disbelief. 'Is that true?'

'I would never have admitted it at the time—I wasn't even conscious of it myself—but I guess I had a few rejection issues. With my mother walking out on me and my father when I was so young I always felt it was somehow my fault. Dumb, I know.'

'Not dumb, Nikos. Just totally unfair and terribly sad.'

'I'd made up my mind I was never going to get married. Then *you* came along. Falling in love with you was a big deal for me. Huge. Far bigger than I ever let on. I didn't believe love existed. Not real, true love. The sort of love that turns life on its head. And then I met you and I thought you'd proved me wrong.'

'Only thought?'

'Yeah, well… After your father died I saw a different side to you. I decided I'd been right all along about the duplicity of women. I didn't react well to being rejected again!'

'I'm so sorry, Nikos. I never meant to make you feel that way. It was just such a terrible time. I was so focussed on concentrating all my energies on looking after Mom that I didn't stop to think how it was affecting you.'

'You were in a bad place and I was making it worse. I tried to back off, but somehow I couldn't do it. And then when you were so pleased to discover you weren't pregnant you touched a nerve. It felt like you were rejecting me as a father.' Nikos paused, feeling a lump in his throat. 'I said some unforgivably cruel things to you. Can you ever forgive me?'

'It wasn't your fault, Nikos. I should have explained my behaviour from the start. Told you about my mother's mental health issues.'

'So why didn't you?' His voice was soft.

'Because my mother asked me not to. She made me promise never to tell anyone, ever. For some reason that was important to her.'

Staring into the depths of her eyes, Nikos suddenly saw the truth. Saw how much Kate had had to cope with. 'Well, her secret it safe with me.' He gently stroked her cheek. 'Am I right in thinking her illness has affected you all your life?'

Kate nodded. 'I've always felt I had to try and be the perfect daughter—balance out her mood swings, try and help her find a way through the dark times. I know she can be very difficult, even when she is relatively well. But she's my mom and I love her.'

'Of course you do. And I love *you* for loving her. But it might take me a bit longer to reach that point.'

Kate laughed. 'Just loving me is enough.'

'Then that's a given. Always and for ever.' He

pressed his lips softly against hers but, feeling the dampness of tears against his skin, pulled back.

'Don't cry, *agape mou.*'

But the tears continued to fall silently, steadily rolling down her cheeks. Reaching out a finger, Nikos tried to brush them away, but her whole body was shaking now with the power of her emotion. Enfolding her in his arms Nikos held her close, absorbing the impact of the tremors, waiting for them to stop.

'I'm sorry.' Finally she pushed back enough to look at him, her eyes shining brightly. 'For so long I've held back my feelings for you and… and now I've finally let go the floodgates seem to have opened.'

She sniffed loudly, then hiccupped and laughed. She bit down on her lip and smiled. And Nikos thought he had never seen a more beautiful sight in his life.

'What made you finally decide to let go?' He cupped her wet cheeks in his hands.

Kate swallowed hard. 'I was at the airport and my flight was delayed, and the longer I waited the more I realised that I couldn't leave.'

'Then I thank God for that delayed flight.'

'Yes.' She smiled against his hands. 'I realised I was walking away from the only thing in my life that mattered. So I phoned Charles Lewis and told him I wasn't coming. I knew I had to explain to you how I felt, even though I was convinced you would throw it back in my face.'

'Oh, Kate…' Nikos felt his insides twist with remorse.

'And I would have accepted that rejection.' Her voice was grave. 'I told myself that as long as I had made you see how much I love you, that was all that mattered.'

'Which makes you so much more courageous than me.' He took a breath. 'Especially after I've treated you so badly, been so harsh to you, pushed you away. And all because I was terrified of my own feelings, I see that now. When I woke to find you gone this morning I wanted to run after you so badly—but even then my stupid pride wouldn't let me.' Regret clawed at his throat.

'I figured I couldn't be any more miserable than I was already, so what did I have to lose?'

The smile Kate gave him arrowed straight to his heart. 'Darling, Kate.' Nikos lowered his head. 'Thank you for being the bravest, most beautiful, most perfect woman in the whole world. And most of all thank you for loving me.'

'You are very welcome.' She touched his lips with hers.

'Would you do me the honour of spending the rest of your life with me?'

'It would be my pleasure.'

Digging into the pocket of his trousers, Nikos retrieved the wedding ring and ceremoniously slid it back onto Kate's finger.

For a moment they both stared at it, and then, taking her hands in his, Nikos linked their fingers together and lowered his mouth to meet hers. And as their lips met, and Kate's eyelids fluttered closed, they both knew that this kiss was very special. Because it was the start of a lifetime of happiness together.

EPILOGUE

'HOW MUCH LONGER?'

'Two minutes, fifty-five seconds.' Laughing, Kate put her phone showing the timer down on the floor beside her.

'Can't we just take a look now?'

'No, we cannot. You've got to be patient.' She held the test stick behind her back.

'Patience has never really been my thing.'

'Then do something to take your mind off it.'

'Hmm…' Nikos gave her a sexy smirk. 'I can think of something, but two minutes fifty-five seconds isn't going to cut it.'

Kate grinned, reaching for his hand. 'Are you nervous?'

'More excited. How long now?'

Kate pushed her phone further away from him. They were sitting on the floor in the bedroom, their backs against the wall. It had been all Kate could do to stop Nikos coming into the bathroom with her, and this was as far as she had been able to banish him.

'Actually,' she started nervously, 'there's something I want to tell you. I've made a decision.'

'Go on.' Nikos squeezed her hand.

'I am going to sell Kandy Kate.'

'You are?' Nikos was visibly shocked. 'You mean if you're pregnant?'

'No.' Kate shook her head. 'Either way. I've spent all this time thinking that Kandy Kate is all that matters, that it's who I am, *all* I am, but now, thanks to you, I know that's not true. I am not that pigtailed girl any more. In some respects I never was. I was always fighting for a part of me that never existed. This is the real me—just a regular New York gal, madly in love with the most wonderful man in the world. You are everything to me, Nikos, and all that matters. Thank you for making me see that.'

'Oh, Kate, I should be thanking *you*. For having the courage to knock down the stupid barriers we had put up, to lay yourself bare like that. I love you so much.'

'And I love you too. More than I can ever say.'

'So...' Nikos fought to control the catch in his voice. 'What will you do, then? I mean, you don't have to do anything, obviously. If you want to be a stay-at-home wife, that's fine by me.'

'I'd like to do more photography, and also get involved in some charity work. It would be good if I could combine the two. And maybe...' Suddenly Kate felt self-conscious. 'Maybe I could help your father in the *taverna*. I know he hasn't always been the father to you he should have been, but I'd like to try and put that right. That's if Marios will have me, of course.'

'*Have* you? He'll snatch your hand off.' Nikos laughed. 'He's still running that place single-handed, flatly refusing to retire, even though I've made sure he's financially secure.'

'It's not about the money. It's his life.'

'You're right. But don't expect *me* to start waiting on tables again.'

'Aw, shame.' Kate touched his cheek. 'You made such a lovely waiter.'

'Yeah, right.' Nikos took her hand and pressed it to his mouth. 'So you'll be swapping one family business for another?'

'Sort of.'

'But definitely no confectionery empire for our unborn offspring to inherit, then?'

'No, definitely not.' Kate's voice was firm.

'I want our children to have the freedom to do whatever they want, *be* whatever they want, free from the shackles of responsibility— What?'

Suddenly she realised that Nikos was staring at her intently, his deep brown eyes shining with excitement.

'You *know*, don't you?'

Kate pulled a nervous face, then gave him a quick nod. 'I feel kind of…different.'

'Like *pregnant*, different?'

She nodded again.

'Come on—hand it over.'

Reaching behind her back, Nikos retrieved the test stick and held it up between them. Kate squeezed her eyes closed. There was an agonising silence followed by a yelp of pleasure, and suddenly she was crushed in Nikos's arms.

'It's positive, Kate!' His voice quavered with awe. 'We are going to be parents!'

Cupping her face in his hands, he laid his forehead on hers and for a few precious seconds they stayed like that, quietly breathing in the magnitude of the moment, before instinctively reaching to find each other's lips for a tender kiss.

And there, locked in Nikos's powerful embrace, surrounded by the immense power of his love for her and hers for him, Kate felt the rush of joy that told her that this time everything was going to work out just fine.

* * * * *

LET'S TALK

For exclusive extracts, competitions
and special offers, find us online:

 facebook.com/millsandboon

@millsandboonuk

@millsandboon

Or get in touch on 0844 844 1351*

For all the latest titles coming soon,
visit millsandboon.co.uk/nextmonth